Ghosts
OF
Vicksburg

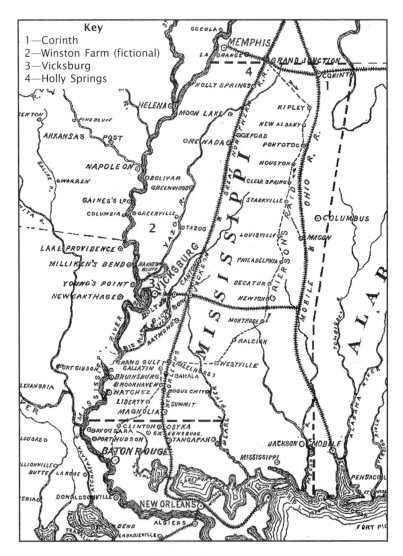

Key
1—Corinth
2—Winston Farm (fictional)
3—Vicksburg
4—Holly Springs

Map of Mississippi

From "Map of Naval and Military Operations in the South-West," *The Soldier in our Civil War*, drawn by Walter A. Lane. This period map shows Mississippi and parts of neighboring Arkansas, Tennessee, Alabama, and Louisiana. The Mississippi River forms the state's western border. Note the pronounced hairpin bend in the river at Vicksburg; at one point the Yankees tried to dig a canal that would bypass the city and allow them safe passage to points south.

Author's Collection

GHOSTS OF VICKSBURG

by

Kathleen Ernst

W̅M̅ WHITE MANE KIDS
K̲I̲D̲S̲ SHIPPENSBURG, PENNSYLVANIA
13

This book is a work of historical fiction.

This White Mane Books publication
was printed by
Beidel Printing House, Inc.
63 West Burd Street
Shippensburg, PA 17257-0708 USA

The acid-free paper used in this book meets the guidelines for
permanence and durability of the Committee on Production Guidelines for Book Longevity of the Council on Library Resources.

For a complete list of available publications
please write
White Mane Books
Division of White Mane Publishing Company, Inc.
P.O. Box 708
Shippensburg, PA 17257-0708 USA

Library of Congress Cataloging-in-Publication Data

Ernst, Kathleen, 1959-
    Ghosts of Vicksburg / by Kathleen Ernst.
        p. cm.
    Summary: When Jamie Carswell joins the 14th Wisconsin Infantry
Regiment fighting in Vicksburg, Mississippi, he finds his cousin Althea
living there, trying to make peace with her past and keep her family
safe during the Union's siege.
    ISBN 1-57249-322-4 (alk. paper)
    1. Vicksburg (Miss.)--History--Siege, 1863--Juvenile fiction. 2. United
States--History--Civil War, 1861-1865--Juvenile fiction. [1. Vicksburg
(Miss.)--History--Siege, 1863--Fiction. 2. United States--History--Civil War,
1861-1865--Fiction. 3. Cousins--Fiction.] I. Title.

PZ7.E7315Gh 2003
[Fic]--dc21

                                                        2003041165

PRINTED IN THE UNITED STATES OF AMERICA

For Stephanie

CONTENTS

ILLUSTRATIONS

ACKNOWLEDGMENTS

I am grateful for the assistance I received from many people while researching and writing this novel. I owe special thanks to Lance Herdegen, Director of the Carroll College Civil War Institute. In addition to many past favors, Lance was kind enough to review a draft of the manuscript. He also provided information about his ancestor Gottlieb Schlingsog of Company I, 14th Wisconsin, who was killed at the Battle of Corinth.

In Vicksburg, I was fortunate to be taken under the wing of Kitty Duncan, a gracious hostess and knowledgeable guide. I also had the good fortune to stay at the Balfour House Bed and Breakfast, where owner Sharon Humble and guide Katy Watt revealed wonderful stories and details about Emma Balfour, her home, and her experiences. Gordon A. Cotton and Jeff Giambrone of the Old Court House Museum kindly answered my questions and identified several photographs. Terry Winschel, Historian at the Vicksburg National Military Park, took time from his busy schedule to share the park's resource file on the 14th Wisconsin Infantry Regiment. Staff at the Corinth Civil War Interpretive Center were also helpful.

My writing circle, as always, let me know when I was going too far astray. Thanks to Eileen Daily, Marsha Dunlap, Amy Laundrie, Katie Mead, and Gayle Rosengren for their companionship and insight. I'm grateful to Renee Raduechel for proofreading the final draft, and to my colleagues at White Mane for their continued support.

Also as always, I want to thank my extended family for their encouragement. Finally, special thanks to Scott, my companion and Webmaster extraordinaire, whose knowledge about the Civil War far surpasses my own.

— CHAPTER 1 —

Near Corinth, Mississippi, August 1862

Jamie

Jamie swallowed hard as sudden perspiration beaded on his forehead. Drat this fog! He was lost. The suffocating gray mist obscured any landmark. And concealed whatever—whoever—was making the hairs on the back of his neck stand erect.

He stood still, clenching his Union Army-issued rifle, and strained to hear the faint sound again. He'd never known that dense fog not only cloaked sight, but muffled hearing as well. Fog like this was rare in northern Wisconsin, where he'd mostly grown up. He was not a stranger to Mississippi; he'd spent every sultry summer near Vicksburg, visiting cousins. But his slight knowledge of the terrain only made his skin prickle. Mississippi was home to more than the Confederates who'd run him through with a bayonet if they got the chance. Mississippi slithered and crawled and buzzed with creatures unknown in the cool dry forests back home, all just as dangerous as the enemy soldiers.

1

Jamie hated picket duty. *Hated* it. Tromping a lonely line in the wee hours of night, while his pards snored safely in their tiny tents, tied his belly in knots. But this choking dark fog—this was the worst yet. One wrong step and he'd lost sight of the last Union campfire. A careful step back in what he thought was the right direction had not provided the comforting glimmer of his army he craved. Nor another step, or another. Now he was hopelessly lost. Was he two steps away from the Union encampment? Half a mile? His best pard, Elisha, slept like the dead, and wouldn't wake to wonder why Jamie hadn't returned when expected.

The damp night smelled of rotting vegetation. The 14th Wisconsin Regiment had skirted a slimy maze of bayous and swamps before making camp. Wetness oozed through the seams in Jamie's army brogans.

A tiny splash pricked the night. What direction had it come from? Goose bumps rose on his skin.

Then a breath of damp air brought the sound of a voice. The snatches of words were unintelligible. But they were unmistakably Southern. He'd spent too many hours arguing with his cousin Althea to mistake that drawl.

"Who's there?" Jamie demanded, his voice ripping open the night. "Who goes there?"

Silence. Heart thumping, Jamie eased the rifle to his shoulder. Eased back the hammer with a trembling finger. Gritted his teeth. Waited.

Crack! A footfall snapped a stick.

And then the night exploded.

— CHAPTER 2 —

Near the Yazoo River, September 1862

Althea

Althea swallowed hard as she pressed her nose against the dining room window. Yankees, bold as brass. *Here.* Noisy soldiers in dusty blue uniforms surrounded the well in the side yard, pushing and shoving like schoolboys. The blue mass filled the yard and the road in front of the house. Their rifles, stacked butts-down in tidy pyramids, glinted in the sun.

Somewhere, Cousin Jamie carried a rifle like that.

"They won't bother us," Caroline said, although her voice shook. Eighteen, she was married and mistress of the house. Althea felt her older sister trembling. Little Nannie, who'd just turned eight, clutched Althea's skirt on the other side.

"They just want a drink," Althea echoed, and managed to sound more confident than she felt. Their small farmstead was isolated, two miles from the closest neighbor; eight from Yazoo City.

The soldiers at the front of the column, who got the first drinks, lounged on the ground while those

3

coming behind waited their turn. Some perched on the snake-rail fence, and one even settled his blue Yankee bottom in the swing Papa had hung for Nannie before he left to serve as a Confederate Army chaplain. "Like they own the place," Althea muttered, as several opened the gate to the kitchen garden and poked hopefully among the squash vines.

"They won't get Smoky, will they?" Nannie whispered.

"George," Althea called softly over her shoulder.

George appeared in the doorway. His eyes were wide in his dark face, but not panicked. "Yes, Miss Althea?"

"You've got that mare well hid, haven't you?"

He nodded. "Way down in the swamp, like Mr. Franklin done told me before he left."

"I wish Franklin was here," Caroline murmured. She twisted the wedding band on her slender white finger.

Althea wished for a lot more than that.

An eternity passed before one of the men bellowed, "Fall in!" The soldiers took up their rifles, and shuffled back into a column. Some passed so close to the window that Althea could see the stripes that drops of water had tracked through the dust on their chins. A few nodded toward the window where the Winston sisters watched. One even tipped his hat. Most of the men ignored them.

"Thank goodness," Caroline breathed. "They're leaving."

But as the column began tramping from their yard, a wiry man with sergeant's stripes on his uniform marched purposefully toward their front porch. Caroline jerked as he rapped at the door. "Oh!"

Althea hesitated, pleating her skirt in her fingers. If they didn't answer, would the Yankee go away? But the man rapped again.

Caroline stared at Althea. "Let's both go," Althea said. "Nannie and George, you stay here."

Althea's stomach curled as they left the room. Caroline's feet stopped moving when they reached the hall. *You're three years older than me!* Althea protested silently. But she forced herself to the front door. The metal door handle felt cool in her clammy hand. She wrenched the door open just as the man rapped again.

"Yes?" she asked, staring at the Yankee sergeant. A prominent forehead, and a mouth that seemed too small for his teeth, gave him the look of a circus monkey. His nose twitched. What if he smelled the cornbread and bacon they'd fixed that morning, half-eaten on the dining room table? Althea blocked the entrance, formidable in her belled hoop skirt.

"Where's the man of the house?" he demanded. His voice was harsh, Yankee—similar to Jamie's. But different too. This man wasn't from Wisconsin, Althea was sure of it.

"Away," Althea began, than instantly scolded herself. They hadn't seen their father or Caroline's husband, Franklin, for months, but there was no call to let this Yankee know that. "They're away at the moment," she added firmly. "We expect the men back any time."

The sergeant sniffed the air like a hound, then put a hand on the door. "I want whatever smells so good. And—" Suddenly he went silent as Caroline joined Althea. Food was clearly forgotten.

Althea felt a familiar hollow twist inside. Even the blamed *Yankees* forgot their names once Caroline came into view!

"You sure are a fine looking woman," the sergeant breathed, staring at Caroline.

Caroline scrabbled for Althea's hand.

"You get along, now," Althea said firmly, tugging Caroline back toward the hall. "You've about drunk our well dry, no doubt. We've got nothing more—"

Thunk. Monkey-face planted one foot against the door, holding it open. One dirty hand reached out. Pressed against Caroline's cheek. Caroline shuddered. A tiny whimper escaped her mouth.

Althea felt the world teeter, as if balanced on a knife point.

Then a war's worth of anger and fear exploded from her: *"No!"* She jerked Caroline behind her, and threw her weight against the door. George appeared from nowhere and slammed into the door beside her. George was fifteen too, and strong. Together they managed to shut and latch the door.

Althea leaned against the door, heart pounding. A locked door meant nothing to the Yankees. Every muscle clenched tight as she waited for a gun butt to crash through one of the hall windows.

Instead she heard only a faint laugh. "Never mind, Miss Dixie," the sergeant yelled. "I'll see you again next time we pass through." Althea dared a peek through starched lace curtains, and saw Monkey-face trotting after the column of blue.

"He *touched* me," Caroline whispered, dropping into the chair by the umbrella stand. "That dirty little Yankee touched me."

"I appreciate your help," Althea said. "But maybe you should stay out of sight from now on."

"If Franklin was here..."

"Well, he's not." Althea pressed a hand against her chest, willing her heart to slow down. She heard Mama's voice in her memory, talking to Franklin Bishop the night he and Caroline announced their betrothal: "You and Caroline have made me very happy. But I'm not a well woman. I need to ask for a promise." Althea had frozen in the hall outside the parlor with the cup of punch she'd been bringing to Mama.

"Mother Winston, I love Caroline," Franklin said. "I'm honored to provide her my care and protection."

"You don't know how much that eases my heart," Mama said quietly. "But these are troubled times. I don't know when the girls' father will be home again. Will you offer Althea and Nannie your protection as well?"

Althea's hand jerked. A bit of punch slopped over the cup and dripped onto the floor.

"Of course, Mother Winston!" Franklin said. Althea could picture his earnest expression. Franklin was Mississippi born and bred. He knew the meaning of duty.

"Nannie will find a man of her own, when the time is right," Mama was saying. "She's pretty, and charming. But take heed of what I'm asking, on Althea's account. She's plain. And any girl who would rather go fishing or read books than...well, I worry for Althea."

The little cakes Althea had eaten that evening turned sour in her stomach.

"Mother Winston, I give you my word," Franklin had promised firmly. "Althea will have my protection. For the rest of her life, if need be—"

"Miss Althea!" George interrupted Althea's unwelcome memories. His nose was pressed against the window on the west side of the front door. "There's more Yankees coming down the road!"

Althea ran to his side. Sure enough, the first blue-coated Yankees of a new column were just marching from the trees.

She turned back to the hall. Caroline's face was still ashen, her eyes wet with unshed tears. Nannie peeked around the door, lower lip quivering.

No more. *No more.*

Althea clenched her hand into a fist. "George, go out the back door and fetch me that carving knife from the kitchen."

He blinked. "The carving..."

"It's on the shelf! Go!" George disappeared. "Nannie, go upstairs to your room, and don't come out until I call you. Caroline—"

"Althea, what are you thinking?" Caroline gasped. "You can't stab a Yankee!"

"I'm not planning to. I'm just going to keep them from bothering us." When George reappeared, Althea snatched the knife and threw open the door.

Althea didn't look at the approaching Yankees as she ran down the porch steps and flew to the well, but she heard their tramping steps. The thick rope that circled through the pulley, used to raise and lower the buckets, felt prickly in her sweaty palm. She heard the approaching rattle and creak of the tin cups and leather haversacks as she began sawing savagely at it with the carving knife. *Drat!* Was this rope threaded with iron? The knife felt dull as wood. The well's stonework cut into her belly, and her corset squeezed her ribs in protest. Strands of the rope popped and splayed. Just a bit farther...

"Hey!" an indignant, thirsty Yankee bellowed.

There! The blade cut through the last strands of rope. The rope whistled through her hands. Both buckets fell into the dark hole with a distant splash. The forlorn pulley swung back and forth, empty. Althea smelled the dust kicked up by a hundred tramping feet as she ran back to the house.

"Ha!" she gasped, when the door was safely shut and latched behind her. "No water for the Yankees!" Her chest heaved as if she'd been running for hours, but an exultant laugh bubbled from inside.

"Althea! I can't believe you did that!" A tiny smile played at Caroline's mouth. "But...we need those buckets too—"

"We can fix it later. For now, there's no reason for those Yankees to stop."

"They are some angry men, Miss Althea," George reported from the window, sounding grim.

Althea peered over his shoulder. The column had halted in front of the house. An officer riding a skittish bay horse left the road and barked something over his shoulder. Two soldiers disappeared from sight, headed toward the well. In a moment they reappeared and spoke to the officer. One of them pointed toward the house. A sudden sheen of cold sweat dampened Althea's forehead as the officer stared at the window, his gaze not wavering even as his mount danced sideways. But after a moment he turned the horse's head back toward the road. "Forward, march!" he yelled.

"They're leaving," she reported. She leaned against the wall, watching as the Yankee soldiers passed the house. Her stomach muscles began to relax. She turned toward the stairs as the end of the column shuffled past. "I'll go fetch Nannie—"

"Miss Althea!" George's voice rose.

Althea and Caroline shouldered him aside. Four Yankee soldiers had left the column and were striding purposefully toward the house. They marched up the front steps without pause, and a violent pounding shuddered through the house. The door shook beneath an angry fist. Caroline screamed.

"Open the door!" an angry voice bellowed. A fresh attack commenced—he kicked the door, this time.

Althea's heart thudded painfully. She winced as she reached toward the quivering door latch.

"Don't let them in!" Caroline begged.

Althea forced her foot to take another step forward. "If I don't, they'll kick the door down."

The furious pounding echoed inside her head. "Give me a chance!" she shrieked through the thick oak panel. The assault paused. Althea's fingers trembled so violently she scarcely found the strength to pull the latch. She stumbled backwards as the door banged open.

Yankee soldiers filled the hall. They smelled of sweat and dust and anger. "Get out," one of them ordered.

"What?"

"Get out!" An iron paw clamped onto Althea's forearm and jerked her toward the front porch. She stumbled over Papa's iron boot scraper. Her knee cracked against one of the graceful white columns framing the front steps. "Ow!"

Then Althea heard Caroline scream again, and blindly launched toward the soldier hauling Caroline out of the house. He swatted both girls aside. Althea stumbled again, landing on flecks of yellow paint kicked from the front door. "Stay outside!" the soldier ordered harshly. Another queer Northern accent. He was missing a tooth.

"What are you doing?" Althea demanded. Caroline began to sob.

"Git *out*!" One of the Yankees dragged George outside by the arm. "What you doing here, boy? You want to come cook for us, or tend our mules?"

"No, suh!"

"Who else is here?" the gap-toothed Yankee demanded. He looked at Althea.

Where was Nannie? Had she hidden herself well? "No one else is here," Althea managed. She lurched painfully to her feet, and tried to peer in the front door. Maybe the men just wanted food.

"That's it?" another man asked from the doorway. He wore glasses, and looked more like a schoolteacher than a soldier.

"Get on with it."

Althea found Caroline's hand and squeezed. "Let them," she whispered, trying to stem Caroline's flood of tears. "Let them take what they want..."

Smoke. She smelled smoke. Jerking away from Caroline, Althea pressed back at the door. One Yankee still blocked her entrance, but she saw the schoolmaster-soldier emerge from the dining room. He held their huge peafowl fly brush, which was blazing like a torch. Althea's heart froze as he touched the dancing flames to Mama's lace curtains at one of the hall windows.

Greedy flames gulped the cotton stitches. Smoke billowed, obscuring the portrait of Grandfather hanging in the hall. More smoke floated from the parlor door.

The marrow in Althea's bones turned to ice. *"Nannie!"* She dove for the front door.

The guard grabbed her arm. "Stay outside, you fool Secesh—"

"My sister's inside!" Althea screamed. Wrenching free, she bounded for the staircase. One of the men bellowed something. Caroline's wails followed her up the stairs.

"Nannie!" Althea cried. "Nannie, come quick!"

Nannie's bedroom door was closed. Althea banged it open. Heavenly Father, where was Nannie? Chest heaving, she scanned the room. The rope-strung bed, covered with Mama's blazing star quilt. The pitcher and basin, white with lavender flowers, on the bedside stand. Nannie's old rag doll, resting in a small wicker rocker. The chest of drawers—there, in the tiny crawl space beyond it. A bit of blue cotton caught her eye.

"Nannie!" Althea jerked her little sister into the open, and caught a glimpse of frightened eyes and tear-stained cheeks. "The house is on fire! Come on!"

A growing haze of smoke had already filled the upstairs hall by the time Althea towed Nannie from the room. Was she too late? Should they retreat?...No. Nothing for it but to plunge back down.

Althea's eyes burned as she started down the staircase. Smoke filled her nose, her mouth. Nannie coughed violently behind her. With one hand on Nannie's wrist, another holding her skirt free, Althea pressed her elbow against the banister to guide their process. She tripped as Nannie stepped on her hem, and skidded down a step, but managed to catch her footing. Almost there.

The western wall was ablaze as they reached the front hall. The fire crackled and roared. Ash and sparks floated through the haze. Heat seared Althea's skin. Each breath burned into her throat, her lungs. The front door, *where was the door?*...

A black hand closed on her arm like iron, and pulled. "This way!" George shouted.

Air. She found air. Warm and damp but blessedly clear. Althea kept her clamp on Nannie's wrist even as her knees buckled.

"Althea—Nannie—oh, thank the Lord." Caroline appeared beside her. "Come away—"

George coughed violently. "Over here, Miss Althea. Git away from the porch."

They stumbled down the porch steps. Althea wiped her eyes and squinted at the road just in time to see the four Yankee soldiers who had fired their house trotting down the road after their regiment. Something bitter rose in the back of her throat.

Caroline, Althea, Nannie, and George huddled beneath a live oak tree and watched the house burn through a mournful veil of Spanish moss. Caroline cried, and Nannie cried, and George kept murmuring, "Oh Lordy be, Lordy be," over and over.

Althea pressed her palm against the massive trunk for support. Spots danced at the edges of her vision. She listened to the fire, saw and felt the waves of heat shimmering from the blaze, and felt as if someone else, some stranger, was living inside her skin.

The white frame house now popping and crackling as the fire consumed it was not large. Mr. Winston had been a minister and gentleman farmer, far from wealthy. Still, it was the only home Althea had ever known. She had said good-bye to Papa on the porch, and accepted friends' condolences in the parlor after Mama died. She had watched from her bedroom window for Jamie to arrive each spring. Somewhere in that roaring storm were the ashes of Grandfather's portrait. Mama's favorite teapot. The quilts Grandmama had stitched. Papa's big Bible. Her copy of *Ivanhoe*. Nannie's doll. Caroline's wedding dress. The old, battered hat George kept hanging by his bed—all he had to remember his father by.

"Oh, Caroline," Nannie wept. "What are we going to do?"

"Heaven help us," Caroline sobbed, arms around her youngest sister. "Heaven help us."

Althea stood apart. When a wall finally collapsed, she tore her gaze away and stared at the empty road. Did the officer who had ordered their home destroyed even wonder what would become of them?

"My throat hurts," Nannie whimpered.

Another section of the house fell in, sending a shower of sparks high above the blackened chimney. Ashes drifted over the clearing, soft as cotton down.

Althea closed her eyes. Her throat still burned. She needed a glass of water. Nannie did too, no doubt...but wait. Their buckets were down the well; the well rope sawed in two.

"Lord God Almighty," Althea whispered, pressing trembling fingertips to her forehead. "What have I done?"

— CHAPTER 3 —

Near Corinth, October 1862

Jamie

Sergeant Neverman looked tired. Still, he beckoned Jamie to a quiet spot under the trees, away from the tents, with a jerk of his head. "What you want, Private Carswell?"

Jamie took a deep breath. "Sergeant...I was wondering if there was any way you could see clear to sending me back to Wisconsin."

The older man's black eyebrows raised like startled crows. For a long moment he stared thoughtfully at Jamie. Company I, 14th Wisconsin Regiment, was settling in to dinner, and shouts and the ring of an ax on wood drifted through the pines with the smell of woodsmoke. Finally Sergeant Neverman shook his head. "You know it doesn't work like that. You can't just wander home. When you enlisted—"

"I know." Desperation pushed the words out. "But I've *got* to get out of the army."

Neverman folded his arms. "And just why is that?"

Jamie scuffed at the brown pine needles. He couldn't tell Neverman about that night in the fog. *Couldn't.* So what could he say? "I've just got to, that's all," he mumbled finally. He'd spent the weeks since that horrible night on picket duty trying to figure out exactly what had happened, and find a way to keep going.

He couldn't do it.

"Jamie, lad." Neverman's voice was unusually kind. "Look, I was worried when you and Elisha joined up, being so young and all—"

"It's not that," Jamie muttered. Crimus, Elisha would be mad as a hornet if he thought Jamie was giving the sergeant cause to think of them as babies!

"The thing is, it's done now. A soldier can't just up and go home because he decides soldiering doesn't suit! I don't have the power to do what you're asking."

Jamie couldn't bring himself to back down. "I thought maybe you could talk to Captain Johnson for me."

Neverman shook his head. "I won't do that. I won't give the captain cause to think poorly of you." He put a hand on Jamie's shoulder. "Listen to me. You did fine at Shiloh."

Jamie sighed, impatient. He knew he was no coward. The 14th Wisconsin's first big battle had been at Shiloh, Tennessee, the spring before. Jamie had seen men so frantic they fired their ramrods instead of loading proper. He'd seen men shirk off the field, and men break down at the sights they saw. Jamie had done nothing heroic that day. He didn't even know if he'd hit a single Rebel. But he'd stood up to it as well as any, and knew he could do it again.

"And you'll do fine the next time, too," the sergeant continued. "You got to see this thing through! If you quit now," his fingers tightened meaningfully, "you'd regret it. It would follow you for the rest of your life. Folks back home would never look past it."

Disappointment welled up in Jamie's chest, and filled his throat. He nodded dully.

"I'm going to forget about this," Neverman said. "And you should too." He gave Jamie's shoulder one last squeeze before walking away.

Jamie stood still. What was he going to do now? He watched a nuthatch search for insects on the closest tree. Finally, because he couldn't think of anything else, he walked back down the company street.

"Hey, Jamie!" Elisha exclaimed. "This is bully beef. Did you get your share?"

"Not yet." Jamie dropped onto the pine needles in front of their little tent beside his friend. An engine had knocked a bull off the tracks while the boys of Company I patrolled a rail line near Corinth that afternoon. They'd marched back to camp with the first meat they'd had to cook up with their corn dodgers in three days.

Elisha employed a bit of cornbread to sop the last juices from the fire-blacked canteen half he used as skillet and plate. "This tastes as good as a threshing dinner."

Threshing dinners. *Home.* Jamie stared at the fire, trying to swallow the lump in his throat.

When he and Elisha were thirteen, their fathers had started hiring them out for the fall threshing ring near Alma, Buffalo County. Elisha spent his summers cutting wheat and rye with a grain cradle, and could

keep up with the men. Jamie, who spent *his* summers
fishing in the Yazoo River and arguing the classics with
Cousin Althea, returned to Wisconsin each fall puny,
the farmers said, as a runt calf. But he was game, and
had earned the fifty cents a day his father expected.

Elisha leaned back on his elbows. "Remember Mrs.
Abernathy's pies? Sour cream-apple, that was the best.
And Mrs. Welti's *roesti* potatoes? And remember Mrs.
Helfinger's *sauerbraten*? Now *that* was good beef!"

"Hush up. You're making me homesick." Jamie tried
to keep his voice light, and didn't succeed. He and
Elisha had run away to join the Union Army in the middle
of threshing season, a year ago, when they were both
fifteen. They'd decided on a day when they'd both
swung the flail one too many times, pounding the ker-
nels of grain free on the canvas sheet spread on
Helfinger's threshing barn floor. Jamie's palms were
blistered and his shoulders ached like fire. Elisha
claimed he was dizzy from walking the slow circle the
men traced 'round the spread sheaves, and half-deaf
from the incessant thumping.

It had seemed like reason enough.

Jamie coughed and waved his hand, pretending
he'd swallowed smoke from their little cookfire, and
turned away. Woodsmoke and tobacco smoke and the
smell of charred beef hung on the damp air. Quiet chatter, hoots of laughter, sudden howls from a group
huddled over a poker game—all normal sounds punc-
tuating the evening. Nothing more, thank God.

"You suppose any folks in Mississippi ever heard
of *sauerbraten*?" Elisha asked. "What do you figure
people at big plantations consider fine eating?"

"First off, there aren't many plantations around here. Too many swampy bottoms, and too much clay in the soil."

"But you've been on some, right? Do your cousins live in a fine place?"

Jamie sighed. "Shoot, no. My uncle's mostly a preacher, and they do a little farming. They're well-to-do, I guess. But they're not gentry."

"Do they have slaves?"

"Just a woman who cooks and gardens, and a man and his son who tend the animals and such." Jamie chewed his lip. "But some of their friends...they had more." Franklin Bishop, the neighbor who'd turned so sweet on Cousin Caroline, was the youngest son in a planter family. The Bishops lived in a large brick house surrounded by Cape Jasmine gardenias and leatherberry bushes, and honeysuckled trellises and screening groves of apricot trees. Beyond that veil were the large steam sugar refinery, steam sawmill, cotton gins, and a double row of squat Negro quarters. Jamie and his mother arrived in Mississippi each spring in time to see hundreds of slaves chopping, and later picking, the endless fields of cotton. Jamie and Franklin were good friends, but Jamie always felt uneasy visiting the Bishop plantation. "Me too," Althea had whispered consolingly. "They just invite us because they go to Papa's church. And if Franklin wasn't the youngest of four sons, they'd never let him come calling on Caroline. He won't inherit much."

"Well, slavery is the South's business, I guess." Elisha slapped a mosquito, then glared at the red smear on his fingers. "These are Rebel mosquitoes, sure enough. Set on drawing blood. Say, Jamie. You think a big battle's coming?"

"Seems like it. I suspect the Confederates would be glad enough to shove us back into Tennessee. And everybody wants Corinth." That dry, dusty crossroads town in north Mississippi would have escaped notice altogether if two major railroads hadn't crossed there. Both armies wanted desperately to control the railroads so they could keep food and other supplies flowing to their troops.

"Yep. Everybody." Elisha's face set into an obstinate frown. "I'm ready to fight hard if it means holding on to the hotel." The Tishomingo Hotel, next to Corinth's rail depot, served ice water—a luxury beyond value to the Wisconsin soldiers enduring their trip south.

Jamie snapped a pine needle between his fingers, considering. For him, this coming battle meant more than hanging on to the Tishomingo Hotel, or the railroads. For more than a month, now, he'd been dragging along his fragmented memories of that night in the fog. Sergeant Neverman wouldn't let him out of the army. Now Jamie had nothing to do but wait for judgment. Would it come on the battlefield?

A shudder quivered through him. Time to change the subject. "How's your foot?"

"Poorly." Elisha grimaced and stretched out one bare foot for inspection. "If you ever need to draw new brogans, ask for a pair with stitched soles. Or if you get a pegged pair, at least make sure the blasted pegs got filed smooth before you sign for 'em."

"It's getting worse, not better," Jamie observed, studying the pulpy sores on the sole of his friend's left foot.

Rail-Road Junction near Corinth

When Edwin Dean of the 14th Wisconsin arrived in Corinth he found "...a Ladies' Seminary, the Tishomingo Hotel and a few small dwellings, Soldiers and camps everywhere, cavalry, artillery, army wagons and mules, and the Negroes of all ages and colors...very much in evidence. My, oh my, how grand and sublime, yet strange, everything looked and seemed to me."

Harper's Weekly, June 21, 1862, by Theodore R. Davis

Elisha sighed. "It's raw," he admitted. "Funny thing is, the top of my head hurts too. I can't figure it. Never heard of a bad foot making your head ache."

Jamie put his cup down. "Don't you remember last night?"

"Remember what?"

"You clod! The sergeant was so angry when you didn't show up for picket duty that he reached in and pulled you out of the tent by the hair."

"He did?" Elisha looked perplexed. "What happened?"

Jamie snorted. Elisha's ability to sleep was nearing legend status in the 14th. This episode would polish it off. "I told the sergeant that I'd wake you up, and get you out there. Don't you remember?"

Elisha thought for a moment. "I remember standing guard...I guess I don't remember how I got there. Thanks, Jamie. I'm sorry you got woke up too."

Jamie shrugged. "It doesn't matter. I wasn't asleep anyway."

"Why not?"

Why not? Jamie stared at the flames. The idea of not sleeping at night was as incomprehensible to Elisha as speaking Swedish. Elisha would never know what it felt like to lie awake for hours. Never know that during full moons, the shadows of tree limbs danced like ghosts on the canvas of his shelter half. Never know how welcome a hoot-owl's call could be in a too-silent night. Never know how it felt to wake, drenched in sweat, after dreaming of a ghost-woman.

"Jamie? Are you well?" Elisha was frowning at him. "You've been acting strange for weeks."

Private Elisha Stockwell, Company I, 14th Wisconsin Volunteer Infantry, original tintype made March 1862

Elisha, who ran away from home at age fifteen to enlist in the Union Army, wrote later, "One of the objections my mother had to my going [to war] was that I was a sleepyhead. When I was tired or had been broken of my rest the night before, and I got to sleep, they couldn't wake me up until I had my sleep out. It troubled me very badly, but [my army friends] knew of my failing."

Courtesy of University of Oklahoma Press

Five weeks and three days, exactly. "I'm just tired." A part truth was better than a lie. Right?

"Is it being in Mississippi? I mean...well, I know that your cousins—"

Elisha was interrupted by the sudden drum beat called the "long roll." Relieved, Jamie put his plate on the ground and jumped to his feet. The boys scrabbled in their little tent and emerged strapping on their cartridge boxes and belts. Rifles in hand, they joined the rest of the boys shoving into ranks.

"I didn't even get my supper," someone grumbled, but Jamie didn't mind. These were the easiest moments of army life: jostling into place, shoulder to shoulder with his pards. He was no more than one insignificant brick in a solid wall of Yankee soldiers. This was how war was meant to be fought.

Two days later Jamie found himself shoulder to shoulder again, this time lying on his belly breathing Mississippi dust outside Corinth. "Steady, boys!" Captain Johnson bellowed, trying to be heard above the din of the Yankee cannons firing over their heads. Jamie squeezed himself into the clay, feeling lost. Elisha, barely able to hobble on his ulcerated foot, had been ordered to stay behind when the 14th Wisconsin Regiment formed ranks that morning. Now Cyrus Creighton lay on Jamie's right side, Jacob Clark on his left—both from Alma Township too, but still.

"It must be ninety degrees," Cyrus grunted. "It's October, for God's sake." Beads of perspiration dotted his face.

"I don't know why we're fighting for Mississippi," Jacob agreed, wincing as a bullet whined uncomfortably close above their heads. "The Rebels can keep it."

Beneath his blue wool coat Jamie was swimming in his own sweat, but he held his tongue. Such Mississippi days were meant for fishing, not fighting. What was Cousin Althea doing, right this minute? Did George have time to go fishing with her, as he sometimes used to do? Was she hiding from Aunt Clarice on the bank of the Yazoo River—perhaps at their favorite spot, a mossy knoll beneath a gigantic old magnolia—idly watching the cork bobber float in the current? Was she curled up in the shade with one of Dickens' novels? Or had the war swept all that away?

At least the Winstons didn't live in Corinth. Thank the Lord for that, for the big fight was about to explode. Many Yankee soldiers were entrenched around the town, but Jamie's regiment had been sent into the woods a half mile away. Captain Johnson deployed his men as skirmishers, moving cautiously forward until they came within range of the Confederate line. After a brief exchange of fire, the captain had ordered a halt in an open farm field. And now they waited.

"All right, boys, on your feet," Captain Johnson hollered. Jamie stumbled to his feet with the others, born along on a wave of obedience when all instincts screamed to burrow in deeper. A fence bordered the far edge of the field, with woods beyond. The Confederates, he knew, would come from those trees.

He wiped sweaty palms on his trousers, hoping the mindless storm of battle would sweep him along as it had at Shiloh. He ducked involuntarily as another shell whined overhead. He wished again that Elisha was beside him. *Come on*, he silently screamed at the Confederates. *Get it over with.* He could smell the tension mounting along the line. Cyrus was shifting his weight back and forth, pulling at his blouse. Jacob's hand moved from his cartridge box to his cap pouch and back. Jamie wiped his hands again. Was it possible for a body to—

"There they are!"

Jamie squinted. Tiny figures appeared in the far woods, their gray and butternut uniforms hard to distinguish at first. Then the first Confederates reached the fence. Swept over it like water over a dam. Jamie swung his heavy rifle to his shoulder.

Captain Johnson waved his arm like a sword. "Give it to 'em, boys!"

The Wisconsin boys squeezed out a ragged volley. The gray tide kept surging. Before Jamie could reload, he felt his line break. Suddenly he was running too, churning down the hill while bullets whistled about his ears. He heard someone scream behind him, but his legs flew toward the trees of their own accord.

The fence on this side was already torn down. After plunging into the dubious safety of the trees Jamie paused briefly, looking for an officer or flag. The woods had become a seething cauldron: Yankees fleeing, other Yankees marching stoically forward, men yelling, shots firing, the artillery still thundering away. A spark had set off a small, smoky ground fire on his left.

"Come on!" Cyrus yelled as he pelted past, angling to the right. Jamie hesitated, looking over his shoulder, and saw the first Confederates burst into the woods behind him. He ran again, darting around trees, leaping over fallen logs.

Jamie tried to follow Cyrus but tripped over a stob and lost him. On his knees, Jamie paused to catch his breath. He was alone. The howls and gunblasts were growing louder behind him. Where was he? How far from his company? His eyes burned and he tried to wipe the sweat from his forehead with one arm. Somehow he'd lost his hat. Maybe he should swing further southeast before trying to find his regiment—

Then the sweat on his forehead turned cool. A butternut figure crept from behind a tree ahead of him. Another appeared, gesturing silently to the men following him. Jamie had stumbled into a Confederate skirmish line.

Jamie's tongue scraped against suddenly-dry lips. He was between two fires.

He quickly eased down to the ground, pressing his cheek against the pine duff. His skin prickled, as if ants were swarming over him. Maybe the skirmishers would swing around him. Go past without seeing his blue uniform. Go past without hearing his heart hammering double-quick. He closed his eyes, hearing the cautious footsteps draw closer. Waited. Waited. Waited.

"Well, lookee here!" a Southern voice cawed. "Looks like we found a Yankee!"

Jamie opened his eyes and saw a dirty toe protruding from a cracked brogan tied together with twine. He looked higher and saw a ginger-haired Confederate soldier towering over him. His blanket roll, secured over one shoulder, showed a coverlet woven in an overshot pattern of red, white, and blue. It struck Jamie odd to see the national colors.

The Confederate pulled the rifle from Jamie's hand. Another man grabbed his shoulder and hauled him to his feet.

For a moment Jamie wasn't sure his knees would support his weight. His heart turned to lead. He'd been captured. He was a prisoner. He would never find his regiment, or catch up with Elisha. He'd likely spend the rest of the war in some prison camp...

Oh. *Oh.* Maybe...maybe this was meant to be. Maybe this was why Elisha wasn't with him. Maybe this was the answer Jamie had looked for ever since that night in the fog.

"I surrender," Jamie said, and let one of the Confederates herd him toward the rear.

— CHAPTER 4 —
Vicksburg, Mississippi, October 1862

Althea

"Are you sure this is a good idea?" Franklin asked.

"No, I'm not sure." Althea was trying hard not to think at all. She concentrated instead on keeping her footing as they walked down toward the Mississippi River on a street so steep that laborers had planted widely spaced cobblestones in the road to help draft animals keep their footing.

A young woman passing in a pony cart awarded Franklin a discreet but admiring glance. Althea's brother-in-law was blessed with blue eyes, a trim figure, and now an officer's uniform too. Endearingly, he never had noticed any hopeful girls but Caroline. Even now, he tipped his hat to the lady without really seeing her.

"I think you've had enough," he told Althea, "I can go to this last place by myself. Let me take you home."

"No." She set her jaw stubbornly. "If he's there, I need to see him."

After reaching level ground along the river, Althea
and Franklin made their way along Levee Street. They
passed foundries, and the long, low rows of warehouses
near the wharves where burly Irish laborers and sweating Negroes loaded and unloaded endless bales of
cotton and huge hogsheads of sugar. Two freight han-
dlers jostled past, and Althea's grip on her brother-in-
law's arm tightened momentarily. A heavy basket hung
from her other arm. She wished she had a third hand
to keep her hem from the muck, and perhaps a fourth
to press a handkerchief against her nose. The mingled
stench of coal smoke, tar, and mule droppings was
thick enough to taste.

The genteel of Vicksburg rarely descended from
the town proper, perched on the hills commanding the
Mississippi River, but the town's lifeblood was below:
the wharves and the railroads. *They* were why the Yankees wanted Vicksburg so badly. Northern troops controlled the upper and lower Mississippi, but as long as
the Confederates held that port, local planters could
still steam their goods to market. Hogs and corn and
Southern troops could rattle by train to the western
shore of the river, ferry across to Vicksburg, then get
distributed all over the Confederacy by rail.

"This way." Franklin steered her toward a small
brick storage building. Two Confederate soldiers patrolled in front of the windowless structure, and a third
stood sentinel by the closed door.

One of the sentries stepped smartly out to meet
them. "Sir!" He saluted Franklin, then nodded to Althea.
"And good afternoon, miss."

"We've been told you have some Union boys from
Wisconsin here," Franklin said. "Do you have a roster?"

The private, a twig of a boy with black hair and blue eyes, hesitated. "Yes, sir. But...but Sergeant Parlee said—"

"Private." Franklin smiled pleasantly. "I'm Major Bishop, serving on General Smith's staff. I'd like to see that roster."

The boy flushed. "Yes, sir."

A moment later Franklin and Althea squinted at a list of names. Althea's stomach heaved. *Yankees*, every one of them. But—there. There it was. She pointed with a trembling finger.

Althea stood back as Franklin returned the list and spoke to the guard. The guard unlocked the door and disappeared inside. A moment later he emerged with a—a scarecrow in tow. Thin, filthy, tattered. The prisoner flinched and raised an elbow to shield his eyes from the sudden midday glare.

"That's not him," Althea whispered, but Franklin nodded and took the prisoner by the arm. "That's not him!" she said again, but something drew her forward. When she was close enough to smell him, she stopped. His eyes, she needed to see his eyes...then she'd know.

Jamie slowly eased his arm away from his face, still squinting. Then his gaze found Althea's. She drew her breath in sharply.

His hazel eyes looked haunted.

She hadn't seen her cousin since the summer before the war started, three years ago. He was taller than she remembered, and leaner. A stranger. In sudden panic she fixed on a tiny crescent-shaped scar by the corner of his mouth. He'd fallen from the live oak tree by Winston Farm when he was eleven, and stood up to his mother's scolding without ever letting on that Althea's dare had sent him climbing in the first place...

Althea reached for him. Jamie jerked away, and her hand dropped. "Oh, Jamie," she gasped, blinking back unexpected tears. "What have they done to you?" She felt Franklin stiffen beside her and remembered that "they" were her own army.

Jamie's mouth smiled. "Hello, Althea. Don't fuss. They've treated us well enough."

An awkward silence stretched between them. Nearby, a man started whistling "Lorena." "You were captured at Corinth?" Franklin asked finally.

Jamie nodded. "I got cut off from my regiment. I was trying to swing back through the woods to find them, and...and got found myself. That was a week or so ago, I think."

"We brought you some food." Althea rummaged in the basket. "A loaf of bread, and a cabbage, and a bottle of water."

Jamie blinked at the offerings, looking confused. "Thanks," he managed after a moment. He uncorked the bottle and took a sip. "They've given us a bit of beef every day, and some cornmeal. And rice, once. But no vegetables. And not enough water. I've been so thirsty—what?"

Jamie knows me too well, even now, Althea thought. He must have seen a flicker of fear, or guilt, in her eyes. She heard again the flames' crackling roar. Her sisters' sobs. All for want of a drink of water.

"I'm going to talk to the guard for a moment," Franklin said. "It's all right for you to move into the shade there," he pointed to several cotton bales and other cargo beside the building, "but don't go any further."

Jamie and Althea retreated to the cotton bales. "Don't get too close to me," Jamie advised, scratching his shoulder. He dropped to the ground and leaned against a bale.

Althea shrugged. "I don't care what anyone thinks." She could feel sweat beading on her neck beneath her bonnet as she perched gratefully on a packing crate.

"No. I mean I'm, well...we call them graybacks." When she frowned in confusion, he shook his head. "Let's just say I'm filthy and leave it at that." He nodded at Franklin. "I didn't know he was an officer. I'm not surprised—I just didn't know."

"He's serving on Major General Smith's staff. General Smith's in charge of Vicksburg's defenses. Didn't you get my letter? Back after Franklin enlisted?"

Jamie shook his head. "Nope. Did you get mine?"

Althea stared at her fingers. "The one when you had just joined up? Yes, it came through." She remembered sitting in the parlor with the letter in her hand, staring at Franklin, feeling first hollow, then sick inside. Franklin was four years older than her and Jamie. But years ago, before Franklin had fallen in love with Caroline, he and Jamie and Althea had spent many summer afternoons fishing for catfish in the Yazoo, or riding like the wind past the canebrakes and cotton fields. Jamie and Franklin, both as close to her as brothers, going into two armies.

"I didn't try to send any more after that. I didn't want to cause trouble for you."

Trouble. She knew all about Yankees and trouble. "Why did you sign up, Jamie?" she demanded. "You didn't have to. Even now, by army rules, you're too young to fight."

"I wish I had it to do over again," he confessed dully, staring at the ground. "This friend of mine back home—Elisha Stockwell, I told you about him—well, one night last fall, they had a war meeting at the log schoolhouse in Alma. Calvin Johnson, this lawyer from Black River Falls, was raising a company. The Black River Rangers. He got everybody all fired up. Me and Elisha had put in a long, hot day, and decided it would be bully to sign up too, and get out of farming for a while. We put our names down but Mr. Stockwell and Pa stood up and said we were too young. Elisha's sister called us snotty little boys, loud enough for everyone to hear. It was humiliating. We worked a few more long days threshing, and...and just up and decided to run off. We caught up with the Alma boys at Fond du Lac, and joined the company."

"It was stupid."

He sighed.

"It was very stupid!" Althea's hands clenched. "I don't hate you, Jamie. But I hate the Yankees. You don't know what they've done."

"I have some idea," he said, so quietly she wasn't sure she'd heard. He sat bent over, elbows on knees, head bowed. Two Negresses carrying laundry baskets on their heads met on the street in front of the prison. They set down their baskets and began a lively conversation. One, wearing a cheerful purple turban, began to laugh. Althea clenched her teeth. Perhaps she could send a message to General Smith, asking him to publish a rule against wearing bright colors and laughing in public.

Finally Jamie sat up and looked at his cousin. Beneath the dirty wool coat his shoulders stiffened, as if bracing for a blow. "What's happened to your family?"

Torn between beating him with her sorrows and protecting him from more hurt, she hesitated for a moment before finally settling on the plain truth. She told him about Papa leaving, hearing the call to minister to the Southern boys flocking to the army camps. About Caroline and Franklin's beautiful and sad wedding, three days before he reported for duty too. Mama dying. Flora, their black cook, disappearing without a word. George's father dying of fever, leaving only George to help the three sisters keep the small farm going. The agonizing summer of 1862, knowing that Yankee troops wanted to win control of the Mississippi River, hearing the distant echoes of Yankee gunboats bombarding Vicksburg, living in mortal terror of seeing enemy soldiers tramping up their road.

Only the final chapter was edited. "Finally, about six weeks ago, the Yankees did come," Althea said, staring at a gambling hall across the street. "And they burned us out. We lost everything but the clothes on our backs, and one mare, and a little silver we'd already buried."

Jamie closed his eyes for a moment. "Lord Almighty, Althea, I'm sorry. What did you do?"

"We survived," Althea said shortly. "We came on to Vicksburg. We have friends here—remember the Greenlees? We're staying with them."

"Greenlees...," Jamie wrinkled his nose, searching his memory. "He's an ice and coal dealer, right?"

"That's right. He's about retired, now. He can't get ice from Illinois anymore." Althea sighed. "They left last summer when the Yankees shelled Vicksburg, but they're back now, and they've been dear to us. And of course Franklin's here, at least for the time being. He looks in on us when he can."

"I'm sorry," Jamie said again. *"So sorry."* His voice shook, and his eyes looked as anguished as she felt. A bit of Althea's own brittle anger eased.

"We're getting by," she said. "Truly. Don't worry about us." That was a gift for the old days, when Jamie steamed down the Mississippi River from Alma, Wisconsin each summer with Aunt Susan, and rescued Althea from the endless feminine drone of musical afternoons and sewing circles.

But he didn't look relieved. "Althea, listen to me. You've got to get out of here. Borrow the money, if you need to, but go."

She frowned. "But where else would we go? I feel safer here than in the country. There are over twenty thousand troops defending Vicksburg."

Jamie shook his head. "No, I mean leave altogether. Travel north. My parents will take you in—"

"Jamie!" Althea couldn't believe was she was hearing. "Go north? Now? I—we—could never do that. We're Southerners!"

"I'm a Northerner, but that didn't keep me from visiting you every summer!"

"But that was before the war! We can't go now. *Wouldn't* go now. No. I wouldn't think of it."

Jamie chewed his lower lip. "Althea...I'm afraid Vicksburg won't prove as safe as you think."

The sun suddenly didn't feel hot...then Althea shrugged off his warning. She trusted her soldiers to protect Vicksburg, as they had before. Jamie had no way of knowing how well fortified the city was. "Yankee gunboats shelled Vicksburg all summer, without taking it! Look up there!" The Confederate flag flew above Vicksburg's gleaming courthouse, which overlooked the entire city. The Confederates had placed artillery batteries at strategic points on that hill commanding the Mississippi River. "The gunboats tried for over two months, and they failed. They left. Vicksburg is safe."

"But—"

"For Heaven's sake, Jamie. Here we come to check on you, after all that your army's done to us, and all you want to do is argue!" Althea rubbed her forehead. She and her sisters wouldn't even *be* in Vicksburg if she hadn't managed to get their house burned down. She didn't want to think about that right now.

His lips twitched toward a smile. "We used to argue for hours, sometimes."

"That was different. The things we argued about didn't matter." How bothered they used to get! Whether *A Midsummer Night's Dream* was a better play than *Romeo and Juliet*. Whether cork bobbers worked best, or wood. That's how they passed their summers: arguing, and laughing, and daring each other to do things they shouldn't. It seemed so foolish, now. "I mean it, Jamie. I don't want to talk about it any more."

Jamie nodded his head, defeated. A finger of new worry plucked Althea's conscience. "Jamie..." She hesitated. "What's it been like? I mean...not being a prisoner, but...before."

He stared at her. Althea felt the intensity of that haunted gaze like a blow, and instantly regretted her question. *No. Don't tell me. I don't want to know—*

"I'm sorry," Franklin said, and Althea almost jumped out of her skin; she hadn't noticed him approaching. "But I think we've strained the guard's patience long enough."

Althea and Jamie shared a glance, and for a tiny moment Althea saw the old Jamie. An odd fragment of memory drifted through her mind: "Is it hard to leave your father and Wisconsin and come down here every summer?" she'd once asked. He'd smiled. "This almighty heat is hard," he'd allowed. "But my father...somehow I never seem to measure up, in his eyes. Down here, I can just be."

I can just be. That's why they'd become such friends, because Althea needed someone to let her just be, too. She needed that now, and she saw that Jamie did too.

But Jamie was in her enemy's army, and a prisoner, and Franklin was waiting.

Jamie stood. "Can I take the food and water inside, do you think? I'd like to share. A few other boys from the Fourteenth got captured too."

Franklin nodded. "I'm sure that would be all right."

Jamie extended a hand, then let it drop to his side. "Franklin, it was good of you to come. I hope it hasn't put you in a difficult position."

"Not at all. You're my wife's cousin. And my friend. It will be a sad day when a Confederate soldier can't see to the welfare of kin. But listen!" Franklin looked hopeful. "I was just talking to the sergeant. He thinks you're going to be exchanged, Jamie. All of you."

"Exchanged!" Jamie blinked, as if Franklin had mentioned sending him to the sun. "Not paroled?" Paroled

meant taking an oath not to fight again. Paroled meant
the end of a soldier's career.

Franklin shook his head. "No. Exchanged."

Jamie's mouth worked for a moment before another word emerged. "When?"

"Soon. Probably within the next few days."

"I see."

A new quiver of worry twisted Althea's stomach.
Jamie didn't look pleased, or even relieved. He looked
horrified.

Her vision blurred again. "Oh Jamie," she whispered,
wiping her tears away angrily. "I hate that things are
like this. I don't know when I'll see you again." Or if.

He gestured helplessly. "Althea...thank you for
coming. It means the world. Give my love to Caroline,
and Nannie."

"I will."

Jamie looked back up at Franklin. "Take care of
her, will you? Take care of them all. This war is no place
for girls—"

"Don't be a ninny!" Althea snapped. Franklin take
care of her? Where had Franklin been when the Yankees came to the Winston farm?

Jamie smiled. Althea blinked back tears as the
guard locked him back into that dark, airless furnace
of a prison cell.

Franklin and Althea didn't speak as he walked her
back toward the town proper. She was drenched in new
sweat by the time they reached Washington Street. Although many Vicksburg residents had fled during the
summer's bombardment, this main business thorough-
fare was coming back to life. In addition to the officers

trotting by on horseback, and boy-soldiers getting their likenesses taken at one of the photographic studios, Althea saw women with market baskets. The smell of roast goose and oyster pie beckoned passers-by from the Washington House Hotel.

But the theater where she and Jamie had seen *A Midsummer Night's Dream* four years ago was closed. The gaslights would stay dark that night, for they weren't safe in wartime. The grocers' display windows were not nearly as enticing as they used to be when Althea was a child, when a trip to Vicksburg was an enormous treat. And a huge black man holding a shovel stood on the corner calling, "Digger for hire, digger for hire." For the right price, he would dig a cave—a crawl space, or an elaborate warren—in one of the bluffs, for families wanting a safe place to hide when the next Yankee shells dropped on Vicksburg.

"*If,*" Althea muttered, as they approached the Greenlees' house.

"What?" Franklin blinked.

"You beat the Yankees off last summer, right? Do you think maybe they won't come back?"

"No, Althea," Franklin said quietly. "They'll be back."

Elaborate wrought ironwork curled around the eaves and balconies of the Greenlees' two-story home on Monroe Street, and lovely gardens sprawled beside and behind the house. Mrs. Greenlee had been one of Mama's dearest friends. Althea remembered long afternoons in the garden, drinking punch and listening to Nannie's latest recitation and inhaling the heady mix of oleander, jasmine, and honeysuckle.

This photograph of a Vicksburg street was taken late in the war. Before the war, Vicksburg was a booming center of trade, and all variety of goods were available in its shops. Citizens were also proud of their city orchestra and a theater company.

Library of Congress

The garden had suffered this year when the Greenlees refugeed to the country during the summer's bombardment. And although not severely damaged, the thick walls were pocked in several places by flying lead or debris. The house no longer looked inviting. But Caroline opened the front door as Franklin and Althea reached the gate. "Franklin!" she cried happily. She hurried to meet him, lovely and delicate as a mimosa blossom. "You were gone longer than I expected. I was worried..."

Althea let the two of them go ahead as she stared at one of the scars in the front wall left from an exploding shell. A sudden shiver cooled the sweat, raising goose bumps on her skin. Jamie was afraid for her.

She wished she hadn't ended their visit by calling him a ninny.

She almost wished she hadn't seen Jamie at all.

In the first dazed hours after watching her home burn to the ground, the only thing Althea had known for certain was that her life had changed in an enormous, profound way. She had ended a chapter, turned the page with her own hand, and life would never be the same. Much as she wanted to, she could never go back.

When Franklin had told them that morning that a few Wisconsin men were among the Yankee prisoners being held in Vicksburg, she had insisted on accompanying him—first to the city jail, where most of them were locked away behind high walls, and then to several empty buildings used for the overflow. *Jamie is a Yankee now*, her brain had insisted angrily. *Jamie is Jamie*, her heart argued. For Jamie's sake, she hoped desperately that she and Franklin would not find him among the prisoners. But a part of her, deep inside, had longed for the unexpected chance to see him.

"I am a fool," she whispered to a hummingbird probing hopefully among the cowslip vines nearby. Underneath that hated blue uniform, Althea had wanted to find in Jamie a talisman of the old days. Something to take her back, even if just for a few moments.

But the old Jamie was gone too. Now she'd have one more frightening image to carry—the haunted look in her cousin's eyes.

— CHAPTER 5 —

The Holly Springs March, Mississippi, December 1862

Jamie

Jamie rejoined his regiment in early December, while it was still encamped in the woods near Corinth. When he and his friend Elisha Stockwell buttoned their two canvas shelter halves together to make a tiny tent, Jamie had an odd feeling of coming home. Jamie lay awake that first night back in camp, listening to Elisha's snores and the faint call of the men on guard. He hadn't wanted to come back to soldiering. But at least he was among pards.

A few days later the 14th Wisconsin left Corinth and set out for Holly Springs, which was the Yankees' supply depot in northern Mississippi and therefore in need of rigorous defense. "Fall in!" the sergeants bellowed. Jamie and Elisha fastened on their cartridge boxes and belts, and their waist belts with cap pouches and bayonet scabbards, and their haversacks. They rolled their blankets inside the shelter halves and rubberized gum blankets and tied the ends tightly, and affixed the rolls over one shoulder. Canteens were slung on last, so they could be easily grabbed, and that was that. Grabbing their rifles, the boys found their place in the column. Jamie had long since whittled his personal belongings down to a toothbrush, some writing paper, and a spare pair of socks.

"I surely am glad you got back," Elisha said as they moved out in a column, four-across. "Leaving Corinth without knowing whether you were captured or killed would have been a sore trial."

By mid-morning Jamie had settled into the rhythm of a long march. The roads they tramped were rutted and dusty, passing mostly through woods and some-times skirting swampy areas and canebrakes. Occasion-ally they passed large cotton plantations, still the subject of disapproving wonder to the small-time farmboys from northern Wisconsin, and once two ibis flying overhead prompted a flurry of gawking excla-mation. Mostly the boys were quiet, though. Jamie let his mind go blank, staring at the blue coat in front of him. The reassuring tromp made by hundreds of bro-gans, and the constant clank and jangle of tin cups and canteens, stilled any unwelcome echoes in his mind.

But shortly after turning from one road onto an-other, when Jamie dropped out of line to relieve him-self, he found himself staring at a small, deserted house closer to the road. Unlike most Mississippi houses, this one had ornate trim. Someone had left a green farm wagon with a broken axle parked beside the house.

"Elisha," Jamie said, when he had caught up. "I think I've been on this road before."

"Hunh?"

"When I was a prisoner. When they marched us to Vicksburg. This looks familiar."

"Well, you're better off this time than last, that's for sure."

Jamie nodded, and tried to fade back into a mindless march. But unease prickled along his skin and he found himself eyeing the roadsides. After Corinth the Confederates had been fair enough to their prisoners, all in all, but had taken a certain pride in herding them under guard. Word had spread, and civilians clustered by the road to watch. Some had simply stared, and a few had offered water silently to the prisoners, after the Confederates had been served. But some had yelled taunts. A little girl in a green striped dress waved a Confederate flag defiantly, with a fierce pride that told Jamie she knew more of war than stories. He had seen several widows too, watching from beneath their black veils, silent as ghosts.

The roadsides were empty now, but the prickling feeling didn't go away. Jamie held his tongue, not wanting to sound idiotic, until Elisha suddenly jerked his head up. "You smell something?" Elisha asked, sniffing the air like a bear-hunting dog.

"Smoke." Jamie caught it too.

"It's the fences," said the boy on Jamie's other side, who was on the outside of the column and had a better view.

They marched into it. Zigzagging fences made of oak rails—the Northern boys called them worm fences—lined both sides of the road, and they were burning. The smoke became stifling and the soldiers' steps slowed. Mutters and chatter and hacking coughs buzzed up and down the line. Jamie and Elisha untied the kerchiefs they wore to keep the sun from burning their necks, wetted them with water from their canteens, and tied them over their noses and mouths. But that didn't keep Jamie's eyes from stinging.

Cyrus Creighton, in the rank in front of him, turned to walk sideways. "Word is, some of the boys in the company ahead of us got taken at Corinth, and they set the fires. They said they got marched over this road on their way to prison. That true? You were with 'em."

"Yes, we did come down this way, but—"

Jubilant shouting somewhere in front of them stayed his words. The lines fumbled to a stop, soldiers bunching in the road. Elisha dropped in the dust, never content to stand if he could sit. Jamie shoved to the edge of the column and trotted forward, keeping a safe distance from the smoldering fences. This wasn't right. Not right. Not right—

He edged past a clump of soldiers who'd already broken out a poker game, past a line of trees separating one field from the next, around a bend. Then his knees turned to custard, and he stumbled to a halt.

A long drive stretched away from the road, lined by two majestic rows of live oaks draped in festoons of moss. At the end of the drive, barely visible, was an elegant two-story house...on fire.

"Whoohoo!" Several soldiers in Yankee blue appeared on the drive, whooping exultantly as they ran toward the road. As they got closer Jamie saw two dead chickens dangling from one boy's hand. A wiry fellow had an armload of sweet potatoes.

The soldiers jammed in the road faced forward again as, accordionlike, the column began to move. "Come on, boys, fall in," someone yelled.

The foragers would have elbowed by if Jamie hadn't stepped in their way. "What are you doing?" he demanded.

"Shut your trap, 'fore I shut it for you," the one holding the chickens scoffed. He was a head taller than Jamie, brawnier, and several years older. He shoved Jamie aside and rejoined the line, grinning.

Where were the officers? Jamie grabbed the skinny man's arm. "There was no call to burn their house!" he hollered.

The other man stopped, squinting. "Say...I remember you. You got took too, at Corinth!" Jamie nodded. "So what's your complaint?" the man demanded harshly. "You got marched over this road, same as me. Treated like a circus animal on parade. A woman from that house spit in my face. Walked right up and spit in my face, and me just sitting on the ground resting!"

"Cooper!" someone called.

As the man hurried to rejoin his friends, a sweet potato fell from his arms. "Keep it!" he called.

Jamie stared at the sweet potato. His head was buzzing. *The Yankees did come,* Althea had said. *And they burned us out.* What had Althea done? Had she done anything at all?

Someone reached down and snatched the potato. "Gotta be quick!" he shouted, pocketing his prize. Jamie hardly noticed. Instead he turned and stared again at the house in the distance. Flames danced from the roof now. Waves of black smoke billowed skyward.

Jamie finally saw a bow-legged man with sergeant's stripes on his sleeve. "Sergeant!" he cried, grabbing the man's arm. "Those boys—they're burning the house!"

The sergeant shook him off. "Get back to your own company."

"But—they're your men! You got to stop them!"

The sergeant planted himself in the dust and glared. "Fall in with your own men!"

Jamie's hand balled into a fist as he watched the man stomp away. He hadn't been able to quit the army. He hadn't been sent home as a paroled prisoner. And now—

"Jamie!" It was Elisha; his own pards had caught up with him.

"I'm coming," Jamie called, but he searched the ranks until he found Sergeant Neverman. "Sergeant," he panted, sidling in step. "This destruction—can't you do something?"

"We're at war," Sergeant Neverman snapped.

"But we didn't come down here to make war on women—"

"Carswell, fall in!"

Jamie couldn't tell if Sergeant Neverman was angry at him, or at what was happening. But either way, the sergeant wasn't going to do anything. Well, then, he'd go to Captain Johnson! Or maybe even—

"Carswell!" his sergeant barked over his shoulder.

"I'm coming!" Jamie yelled, although his feet seemed to have taken root. Captain Johnson was somewhere ahead. He'd seen what was happening. If he was going to stop it, he would have done it by now.

Simmering with frustration, Jamie squinted through the haze of smoke from the fence rails. Someone else was flowing down the drive. A woman...no, a girl, maybe his own age. Or Althea's. She wore a pale blue flowered dress over one of those hoopskirts, with a pretty white lace collar. Her face might have been pretty too, if it hadn't been twisted up.

"Why?" the girl screamed as she drew closer. The rest of the soldiers were passing by, ignoring her, so she finally locked her anguish on Jamie. "Why?" she begged him, tears streaming down her face. She sagged to the ground and that huge skirt belled out like a big blue puddle. "Why?"

Someone grabbed Jamie's arm. "Come on," Elisha muttered. "There's nothing you can do."

"Oh Lord," Jamie whispered. A faint breeze stirred the melancholy festoons of moss framing the girl in blue.

"Come on!" Elisha pulled harder, dragging him away. Jamie stared over his shoulder until the girl was lost from sight.

Jamie saw more foraging on that march. More houses burned. His horror boiled down to a ball of lead in the pit of his stomach. "It's not right," he said, over and over. "It's just not right."

"It's harsh," Elisha agreed soberly.

"I didn't join up to fight women and children!" Jamie shifted his rifle. It got heavier by the mile on long marches.

"I didn't either."

They shuffled another mile in silence. Jamie's canteen was empty, and dust sifted into his nose and mouth with every breath, and he figured he'd rather die of thirst than stop at some Southern woman's well. "Elisha," Jamie said finally. "Do you still believe the Union must be preserved? After everything we've seen?"

"Sure," Elisha said, so promptly Jamie wasn't sure his friend had given much real thought to the question. "Don't you?"

Jamie remembered attending that recruitment meeting, back in Alma, and listening to the officers talk about The Union with a glory in their eyes. Jamie had felt swept away, the way folks talked of being swept away at church meetings sometimes. "Yes," he said slowly. "I do. When the officers talk about saving the Union, it sounds so—so good. Noble, almost. But war's meant to be fought amongst the men. I can't countenance getting women twisted up in it."

"Well...I guess it teaches them a lesson."

That wasn't good enough. Jamie wiped sweat from his forehead with a dusty sleeve. "Elisha..."

"Mmnn?"

"Remember I told you my cousin Althea came to see me in Vicksburg?"

"She brought you food."

"She got burned out. Her and her sisters. Some Yankees came and did it." Jamie hadn't told Elisha that part of the story. Something about Althea—maybe that new look in her eyes—made it hard to talk about. There was so much he hadn't sorted through yet.

Elisha exhaled in a long, low whistle. "Oh. No wonder—I mean, well...look, I know it's hard for you being in Mississippi. With family here."

If only that was the hardest part of it! "She had this look about her...I guess I can't explain it, since you didn't know her before." Jamie shook his head. He had wanted so badly to reach out to Althea, that day outside the makeshift prison in Vicksburg. Ached to have a moment, just one moment, of the comfortable acceptance they'd always felt together. But he didn't deserve that anymore. Besides, the look in her eyes had frightened him.

"A spring!" someone bellowed, and orders to fall out came down the line quick. Edgar Houghton volunteered to take canteens to the creek, down a hill through some woods, and Jamie gladly surrendered his. The Wisconsin soldiers dropped by the side of the road to rest. A few scrabbled for bits of hard crackers to gnaw, and a few more flopped belly-down for a quick game of dice. Jamie lay on his back and covered his face with his hat, and tried to forget the girl in blue.

"What was it like, all those summers?" Elisha asked slowly. "Coming down here. Being around all the slaves, and it being so infernal hot, and nobody to talk to but girl cousins? I don't remember you speaking about much but fishing."

Jamie pulled his hat aside and squinted at Elisha with one eye, astonished that he wasn't already asleep. "There was good fishing," he acknowledged. "But it wasn't a bother, just having girl cousins. Althea and me always hit it off."

"Is she pretty?"

Jamie snorted. "The time's not quite right for you to be thinking of sparkin' any girl, much less Althea! Pretty?" He considered. "Not the way some people think. Aunt Clarice—that was my mama's sister—was forever telling her to take more care with her hair, or her clothes."

"I do like a pretty girl," Elisha sighed.

"My oldest cousin, Caroline, she's a beauty. Everybody always remarks on it. And the little one, Nannie,

she's cute as a kitten. She's got a prodigious memory..."
Jamie closed his eyes again, drifting back to the parties
he'd attended. Every hostess asked Caroline to sing or
play the melodeon, and Nannie always brought thunderous applause after prettily reciting Tennyson or Lear.
Althea sat stiffly through these performances, making
funny faces if she caught Jamie's eye. Had she felt left
out?

"Anyway, Althea's too smart for you," he added,
wanting to shake off that memory. "She loves books
with a passion." Aunt Clarice had fretted about that
too, but Althea's father had shielded his middle daughter on that count: "Leave her be, Clarice," the soft-spo-
ken preacher would say. "A wise man will one day be
happy to have an intelligent woman as his wife."

Jamie liked remembering Althea this way. Talking
about the old days blotted from his mind the hollow-
eyed girl who'd visited him in Vicksburg. "Althea was
always impetuous," he said. "That was the only thing I
ever heard Aunt Clarice truly scold her for—"

A gentle snore from his pard stilled his tongue.
Oh, well. Some other time. He'd tell Elisha about the
dares. Like the time Althea had dared Jamie to take
the path through Tom's Bayou at dusk...

Jamie jerked upright. Now, why had he thought of
that? That had been years ago. He'd been game—at
least until he was out on his own in the splashing,
steaming jumble of blackwater and cypress trees. But
he had grown more confident, and his nerves had
started to settle. Then one foot lost the path, and he
sank knee-deep in ooze. When he tried to jerk back to
safe ground, he slipped and fell. Wild panic propelled
him torpedolike back to solid earth, and he turned tail

and lit out for the Winston farm as fast as prudence allowed.

Later, when his heartbeat had calmed and his breathing slowed, he tried to name his fear. The terror hadn't been prompted by thoughts of stumbling over cottonmouth snakes and alligators, or losing the path altogether, although either of those might have happened. But that instant when his foot should have struck hard earth, and didn't, he knew for the first time that real things, solid things, could disappear.

He felt that way now.

Jamie wiped sweat from his forehead, remembering that girl in blue. Remembering Althea's wooden voice: *The Yankees did come. And they burned us out.* And worst of all, remembering that woman in the fog—

"Fall in!"

The boys of Company I, 14th Wisconsin, scrambled to their feet. Jamie stood more slowly, then nudged Elisha with his foot. "Elisha. Elisha! Get up, we're moving out."

Elisha rubbed his eyes, then looked around. "Is Ed back yet?"

"Nope."

"Wouldn't you know it! Now I've got to tote his gun, too. I said I'd hold it while he took the canteens to the creek."

"He must be coming," Jamie said, as they fell into ranks. "He'll catch up."

But Ed Houghton, who'd gone to the little stream with two dozen canteens, didn't catch up. Elisha complained mightily about hauling two rifles. "Oh, give me that," Jamie said finally, wishing like anything that he could share his load too.

— CHAPTER 6 —

Vicksburg, December 1862

Althea

"Althea, dear," Mrs. Greenlee said hopefully. "Don't look so glum. It's Christmas Eve! And we're going to a party. Dr. and Mrs. Balfour have marvelous parties!"

"Unfortunately, I don't have a party dress," Althea said. Mrs. Greenlee's face fell. The older woman's shoulders were bowed above her corset, and when she cringed from Althea's retort, she put to mind a turtle retreating back into the shell. Althea sighed, regretting her hasty remark. It was odd...she'd never enjoyed dressing up in silk and finery. But watching *others* dress up when she couldn't wasn't much fun either. Her own best dress— and the gold bracelet Papa gave her for her fifteenth birthday, and her earrings, and the beaded net Mama had made for her hair—had burned in the fire.

Althea, Caroline, Nannie, and Mrs. Greenlee were crowded into one of the guest bedrooms where the girls had found refuge when they arrived in Vicksburg three months earlier, while Mr. Greenlee patiently waited downstairs with his pipe and the latest edition

of the *Vicksburg Citizen*. Mrs. Greenlee's thin face,
framed by the wings of gray in her dark hair, remained
so distraught that Althea spread a smile on her own.
She'd perfected that skill in the past few months.

"Never mind," she said, and kissed her hostess's
cheek. "It doesn't matter. Truly."

"You'll have a good time anyway, I predict."
Caroline leaned closer to the mirror and fiddled with
the short sleeves on the dress Mrs. Greenlee had loaned
her: corn-colored silk trimmed with black lace around
the neckline and sleeves and skirt. Caroline was slender as a tapestry needle, and fit into the dress with
just a bit of alteration.

"Of course," Althea murmured. After all, her green
plaid cotton—a gift from one of the Greenlees' neighbors—was freshly washed and ironed. The worn spots
near the hem were scarcely noticeable. I have no right
to mind, Althea thought. I ought to be on my knees
thanking Mrs. Greenlee for providing silk dresses for
Caroline and Nannie.

"I thought you didn't care about pretty things anyway, Althea," Nannie said. She was looking in the mirror too, twisting so her shin-length hoopskirt spiraled
back and forth. Nannie was small enough that Mrs.
Greenlee had been able to cut down another silk dress
and make it over for Nannie: blue silk trimmed with
white point. New lace-trimmed pantalettes peeked from
beneath the skirt as she swayed, admiring herself.

"I think," Althea said, "I'll go down and wait with
Mr. Greenlee."

Cold rain pounded on the carriage roof as Mr.
Greenlee's driver drove them to the party. I should have

stayed home, Althea thought, as he maneuvered the carriage to the Balfours' back door, where they could dash quickly inside. Dr. and Mrs. Balfour greeted them in a hall graced with a magnificent elliptical staircase. Althea couldn't remember feeling so dowdy.

It was an elegant party, considering the wartime shortages plaguing the South. The parlors in the graceful brick house on Crawford Street grew warm and noisy as civilians wearing their finest took the opportunity to thank the Confederate officers in attendance—even General Martin Smith had come—for their continued protection. Local merchants couldn't get lamp oil anymore, or oranges, raisins, dates, and many other staples. But a wealth of candles cast a magical glow. A buffet table with twelve leaves in place groaned under platters of turkey, goose, oysters, applesauce, squash, and sweet potatoes. Althea filled her plate, then managed to find a dim corner where she could enjoy it. Although not slim enough to fit into one of Mrs. Greenlee's gowns, she'd lost weight since the fire. She never sat down to a meal without remembering that only the charity of her mother's old friends kept food on her plate.

After dinner the guests sat in tight rows, the ladies' skirts blooming like inverted flowers, for entertainment. Nannie recited "Lady of Shalott" without a fumble. "What a darling!" a lady sitting behind Althea whispered. "She's homeless, you know," her companion whispered back. Althea took a deliberate sip of punch.

A short while later, Caroline played "The Jefferson Davis Grand March" on the pianoforte. "Mrs. Bishop represents all that is good and fine in our Southern

women," an officer murmured admiringly. "I am reminded of what we are fighting to protect," his friend
murmured back. Someone behind Althea sniffled au-
dibly, and the woman beside her dabbed her eyes with
a lacy handkerchief.

Althea tried to swallow a sudden lump in her
throat. Drat! Patriotic music didn't usually make her
weepy. Maybe it was because Papa hadn't been able to
come home for Christmas. She hadn't known whether
to hope for or dread his visit—how could she look him
in the eye, after getting their house burned to the
ground?—but when the letter came, saying he couldn't
leave his regiment, she'd been overwhelmed with disappointment.

Caroline smiled and took her seat amidst enthusi-
astic applause. Althea reached for a handkerchief, then
realized she didn't have one.

She didn't have even a handkerchief to call her
own.

Since the fire, Althea had been living in a skin
brittle as the thinnest glass. At that moment she feared
that if she didn't escape the press, and find a private
corner, she would break into a million tiny shards. She
confronted the barricade of crinolines and fluttering
fans and gleaming military boots with as much com-
posure as she could muster. "Excuse me," she whispered to the woman beside her, trying to step over the
enormous balloon of green silk filling the aisle. "Par-
don me..."

She was almost free when Mrs. Balfour, who'd been
introducing the next musical selection, stopped her
flight. "Ladies and gentlemen, excuse me. I see Althea

Winston near the back, and I'd like her to join me for a moment."

Splink! Althea's glass shell cracked. She froze as heads swiveled in her direction. Don't do this to me, she tried to tell Mrs. Balfour with her eyes. But her hostess smiled and beckoned. Somehow Althea managed to propel herself to the front. She stood before the rows of guests like a prisoner on trial.

Mrs. Balfour took Althea's hand. "My friends, during this wonderful interlude, you've heard Nannie Winston recite, and Caroline Winston Bishop play the pianoforte. Both of these lovely young women are a tribute to the South. But you may not have met the third Winston daughter, Althea."

The glass cracked a little further. Althea wondered if it was possible to die, actually fall down and die, from shame and mortification.

Mrs. Balfour squeezed her fingers. "As some of you know, the Winstons are our guests in Vicksburg. They came here as refugees, after the Yankees burned their home. But you may not know all of the details. One day in September, a column of Yankees visited the Winston home near the Yazoo to use their well. When one of the soldiers crudely offended the sensibilities of Mrs. Bishop, Althea decided to take action to protect her sisters. In the face of an oncoming column, Althea disabled the well in hopes that the invaders would leave them alone."

A murmur rippled among the guests. Althea focused on the parquet floor—light and dark diamonds.

"Well, instead of leaving these defenseless young women in peace, the Yankees forcibly evicted them from their home and set it afire. Little Nannie might have perished if Althea had not braved the flames. Ladies and gentlemen, I think we should take a moment to honor a true daughter of the South."

Althea blinked as the guests applauded. She felt as if she'd been in the sun too long without her bonnet. What were they thinking? She wasn't brave. She had been impetuous. Her impulsive act had cost her family their home, and almost killed Nannie in the process.

But the gentlemen rose to their feet. "As long as our women show such spirit, the South can never fall!" a lieutenant called. "Huzzah!" shouted someone else. The applause swelled to fill the room.

Althea's confusion slowly faded to wonder. And for the first time since that horrible September day, she thought that maybe, just maybe, she deserved to go on living.

Servants cleared the chairs away and three more musicians joined the pianist in the corner. Althea backed away from the dance floor, content to watch. Soon couples were circling in a glorious, whirling waltz. Twelve-foot mirrors between the windows reflected light from a dozen candelabras. Strauss had never sounded finer. The ladies looked especially lovely, their graceful skirts swaying in the soft light. The officers looked gallant and resplendent in their gray uniforms, trimmed with gold braid and gleaming buttons. Caroline twirled by in Franklin's arms, laughing—laughing!—for what was surely the first time since the fire.

A memory flitted through Althea's mind: a soft spring evening ball, at a plantation near Yazoo City, the first time Franklin had danced with Caroline. Jamie and Althea had exchanged a knowing glance, sorry that Franklin had come to value romance above fishing, but at least relieved that he'd looked no farther than Caroline. Watching them dance now, four years later, Althea sighed. Where was Jamie this Christmas Eve? He should never have enlisted. Jamie was the one who needed to go home to Wisconsin—not just because of the look she'd seen in his eyes, but because certainly that lieutenant who'd spoken up earlier that evening had been right. The South was going to prevail. Union gunboats had rained shot and shell on Vicksburg for forty-seven days the previous summer, and the gunboat captains had finally given up and steamed away. Now here were the good people of Vicksburg, smiling, laughing, dancing. Undaunted.

The clock had struck midnight, and Nannie had fallen asleep in her lap, when Althea heard a sudden commotion in the hall outside the ballroom. Women backed away as a drenched mud-spattered soldier stalked into the room. He paused, searching the crowd, then pushed through the dancers to General Smith. Other couples faltered to a halt as the messenger whispered into General Smith's ear. The general's face turned ashen. Althea felt her hard-won contentment slide away in one sickening lurch.

General Smith held up a hand, and the wavering musicians let their instruments slide discordantly into silence. "This ball is at an end," the general announced grimly. "The enemy are coming down the river."

— Chapter 7 —
The Louisiana Bayou Expeditions, January 1863

Jamie

Eighty-eight Yankee gunboats and troop transport ships were steaming south toward Vicksburg that night. A citizen upriver saw them pass and managed to telegraph a message, giving the Confederates time to strengthen their defenses. The Yankees waited until December 28 to strike against Vicksburg at the Chickasaw Bluffs, six miles north of the city. Southern artillery sent a withering bombardment of shell down upon the Yankee soldiers struggling through the wild maze of bayous. The next day a few Yankee soldiers managed to reach the foot of the bluffs, but were pinned down by ferocious fire from above. They frantically scooped out little burrows in the bank with their hands, and hid there until nightfall provided a safe retreat.

Jamie wasn't in the battle at Chickasaw Bluffs, but when he heard about it, he felt sick. His own army lost almost two thousand men in the disastrous attempt to reach Vicksburg from the north, and estimates placed Confederate casualties at less than two hundred. "Why don't our generals just give up?" he muttered to Elisha, in the privacy of their little tent.

Elisha looked horrified. "Give up? We need Vicksburg. We can't win the war without Vicksburg."

At what cost? Jamie wondered, and rolled on his side so Elisha couldn't see his face. And how were his cousins faring in all of this? Were they still in Vicksburg? He didn't know what to wish for. Confederate raiders had taken the Union Army depot at Holly Springs, destroying one and a half million dollars worth of goods; and some Southern cavalry had torn up railroad tracks near Jackson, cutting the Union provision lines. The loss of Union supplies meant the Yankee soldiers ranging through Mississippi were hungrier. And angrier.

"This is not—" Elisha drove his shovel blade into the ground, "what I—" he tossed a scoopful of earth aside, "enlisted for."

"At least it keeps us warm." Jamie used his brogan to push his own shovel into the soft soil. They labored in a long line of Yankee soldiers, stripped to their blouses. The latest rainfall had tapered off, and the earth steamed as weak winter sunlight poked through the bare tree limbs overhead.

"I prefer the cold."

"I don't think this will work anyway," Jamie grunted.

Elisha paused to wipe sweat from his eyes, leaving a smear of slimy mud across his forehead. "Well, you got to give General Grant credit for trying. Last summer showed that we can't take Vicksburg by bombarding it from the river. That mess of a battle at Chickasaw Bluffs showed we can't get infantry through north of the city. This *could* work." He slapped irritably at a hovering ball of gnats. "Although at times I do suspect that this is nothing more than a plan to keep us too busy and tired to notice we're not going anywhere."

"I'm just glad to be out of Mississippi." New orders had brought the 14th Regiment into camp on the Louisiana side of the Mississippi River. General Grant was trying to create new approaches through the web of bayous, canebrakes, bogs, and rivers lacing the countryside. The 14th Wisconsin was one of the regiments detailed to dig a canal in hopes of diverting the Mississippi River into a new channel. If successful, the Union Army could steam south in Louisiana and reach a safe crossing point to Mississippi well below the range of the Southern artillery planted at Vicksburg.

Ed Houghton was trundling by with a wheelbarrow of planks, which the boys used to stand on in the swampy bits, and overheard Jamie's remark. "Don't see much difference," he observed. "Mississippi, Louisiana, they're both just a mess of swamps and rain."

"Those crawdads Jamie caught weren't half bad," Elisha allowed. "You should have tried 'em, Ed."

Ed snorted. "Anything that looks like that wasn't meant for eating. This place breeds unnatural creatures. Did you see that alligator the boys shot this morning?"

"How much snow you figure they got back home?" Elisha asked.

"Well, enough to go sledding, I know that," Ed said.

Elisha leaned on his shovel. "My pa was fixing to get a new sleigh the winter I left."

"I'm going to get me a racing cutter when the war's done with." Ed grinned. "And a fast Morgan horse to pull it."

"Remember Abe Brody's cutter? And that time he raced on that straight track north of Alma and almost crashed into Widow Higgins when she was coming home from choir practice?"

Jamie kept digging while his friends gave in to homesickness. A Wisconsin winter seemed no more real than the moon. He sometimes wondered if he was destined to die in one of these southern swamps. Maybe an alligator or snake would get him. And lots of boys were dropping of typhus and diarrhea, some just throwing down their blankets in the mud and curling up with the shivers—maybe he'd go like that. It could come from a musket ball too, though. No telling when the Confederates might hit, or even some local civilian creeping through the swamp. He wondered if he'd scream if he got shot...and if someone would hear him, and later be haunted by the sound—

A mule nearby brayed shrilly, and Jamie about jumped out of his skin. Crimus! he scolded himself. It was nothing more than another wagon mired hub-deep in the mud, and some of the boys trying to urge the mule team on.

Jamie stabbed his shovel into the earth, hoping his friends hadn't noticed. Stay steady, he told himself. At least he wasn't in Mississippi. At least this kind of labor wore him down as even hard marching couldn't do. With a clod of luck, he'd roll up in his blanket that night so exhausted that even the echoes of an endless, gut-stabbing scream couldn't reach through his sleep.

— CHAPTER 8 —
Vicksburg, February 1863

Althea

"Althea dear, we're delighted to have you join us!" Mrs. Loring chirped as she met the newcomers in her front hall. She was a gaunt woman who balanced a pair of spectacles precariously on her very long nose. Mr. Loring owned a cotton plantation up the Yazoo River, and several warehouses near the Vicksburg docks, and those afforded the family a gracious Greek Revival-style house on Oak Street whose front lawn stretched down to the river. A shell launched by the Yankees across the river had crashed into one corner of the house earlier that winter, leaving a yawning hole in the floor of the dining room. But the Lorings boarded over the broken window, and locked the dining room door, and went on as usual.

"Hello, Mrs. Bishop!" Mrs. Loring kissed Caroline's cheek. "And Mrs. Greenlee...and here's my sweet Nannie!"

She's not *your* sweet Nannie, Althea thought sourly, but Nannie wrapped her arms around Mrs. Loring's neck for a hug.

"I've been telling Althea all winter what fun we have," Caroline said, which did nothing to improve Althea's mood.

"And it's all for a good cause." Mrs. Loring waved them into a side parlor. "Althea, let me introduce you to the group."

Twenty-some women and girls had already gathered in Mrs. Loring's sitting room, squashed onto the sofa and perched in those dining room chairs that had survived the shell. "We've been meeting since the war began," Mrs. Loring said proudly. "We've made flags, and knit socks, and prepared bandages...so many things to keep us busy!"

Althea nodded to those she already knew, smiled politely at the others, and tried not to panic. It wasn't, as she'd told Caroline and Mrs. Greenlee over and over, that she didn't want to help The Cause. There were just few things she hated more than being handed a needle and thread.

"Didn't you bring something?" one of the other girls asked. "We can't get fabric, you know."

"I brought an old dress to cut up," Mrs. Greenlee said quickly, while Mrs. Loring hushed the girl in a loud whisper: "They were burned out! Didn't you know?"

"I'm Mrs. Martin," an older woman said. Lines near her mouth gave her a sad look, so when she smiled, her whole face lit up. "What would you like to work on? Some of the ladies are making quilts for the hospital, and some are making nightshirts."

Caroline quickly accepted a row of quilt blocks to stitch together, and Nannie plopped prettily on a cushion near the fireplace to hem a nightshirt. "I thought perhaps...that is, I was wondering if you might like me

to read aloud while you sew," Althea said brightly. "I've
a good voice for reading."

Several of the women exchanged glances. "That's
a sweet offer," Mrs. Loring said. "But...that would make
it difficult for the rest of us to chat, wouldn't it?"

Drat. That had been her best idea. "Ah. The thing
is...I don't sew particularly well," Althea admitted.

"Oh, this is simple. Here, I've got the pieces cut
out already." Mrs. Martin smiled again. "I hope some
poor boy appreciates my best ball gown." This particular nightshirt had been cut from rose-colored silk. Many
of the other shirts-in-progress showed delicate floral
prints or paisleys. Vicksburg had once boasted several
fine drygoods stores, but the storekeepers had gone
out of business. The Yankees controlled so many railroads and rivers that things like shoes and dress-goods
and hats were impossible to find.

Althea accepted the sewing. She *wanted* to be helpful. Truly. Franklin was serving in the Confederate Army,
and Papa too—she'd do *anything* to support them. If
only the silk didn't fray so easily. If only the thread
didn't tangle. If only—

"Althea, darling." Mrs. Loring leaned over her shoulder. "The seam would be stronger if your stitches were
smaller."

I should have listened when Mother scolded me
about sewing, Althea thought, as she tried again.
Caroline was chattering happily, her needle flashing.
Nannie finished her hem and asked for another.

Althea pressed her lips into a tight line. Why hadn't
they accepted her offer to read? Really, all the news
the ladies hashed over was bad: a little boy killed by a

shell, a cow stolen, a horrid storekeeper profiteering on smuggled goods while good citizens went hungry.

Althea's sweaty fingers left damp blotches on the silk as she tried to fit the sleeve into the armhole. Dratted thing! It buckled and puckered. I *will* do this, she thought grimly. Some poor wounded soldier in the hospital won't care if the stitches aren't quite even. When the sleeve was finally sewn in place—only two needle-pricks later—she wanted to crow with triumph. There!

Althea put the shirt aside, rubbing her fingers. A servant had laid out plates of cornbread and molasses cookies, and Althea helped herself. She was nibbling, and admiring a framed print of two kittens stalking a fish bowl, when she heard low voices behind her.

"We can rip it out later," Mrs. Loring murmured.

"Poor dear. Didn't her mother teach her?" another woman murmured back.

Althea didn't need to turn around to know that the women were looking at a half-finished nightshirt stitched clumsily of rose silk.

Her face grew warm. The skin between her shoulderblades prickled from the pitying looks she imagined directed her way. Then she put down her plate, walked quietly through the parlor, found her shawl on a peg near the front door, and left.

Once outside she felt an enormous sense of free-dom, even though she walked very quickly in case Caroline should come chasing after her. But Caroline didn't come, and Althea's steps slowed again. What had she done? Stupid! She'd been impulsive. Running away didn't solve anything! She'd just given all those women even more to cluck about. When they got home Caroline would scold, and Mrs. Greenlee would fret. Nannie would probably offer to show her how to sew properly...which might very well, Althea thought, send me shrieking into the street.

She paused at the corner of Cherry and Jackson Streets, waiting for a wood hauler to clatter by. It was just so hard here! This wasn't *home*. Home was the Winston Farm near the Yazoo, with the freedom to ride and roam. Here, Caroline and Mrs. Greenlee both felt responsible for her.

The streets were crowded with soldiers, and it seemed to take a long time to walk the six blocks to the Greenlees' house. When she reached the front walk she paused. Mr. Greenlee was probably inside, and she didn't want to explain why she was home so soon. Althea chewed her lip, then slipped around the house to the back garden.

The day was damp but mild, for February. A squirrel skittered away at her approach, but the garden wasn't deserted. Althea found George clearing brush away from the neglected beds around the basin that had once held goldfish. "Hello, George. What are you doing?"

"Just keeping busy, Miss Althea. Ain't much work for me in the house. I'm figuring we might want to plant some sass back here, come spring. Could come in handy."

"That's an excellent idea." Althea sank onto the bench.

George tossed some dead leaves in a big willow basket. "You're back early. Mr. Greenlee done said he didn't expect you ladies back before suppertime."

Althea sighed. A mockingbird hopped closer, then flitted away. "You're a very handy person, George."

"What's that, Miss Althea?"

"I mean, back at the farm, you did everything after your father died. Planted the garden. Got in the hay, and corn. Kept the animals fed and the stable clean. I've seen you sharpen a scythe and make new soles for a pair of shoes and hew out a shingle."

George looked wary. "Is there something you're needing, miss?"

Althea rubbed her arms. "No. Not really. I guess— I just mean, I appreciate all you do. I don't suppose you're particularly happy here in Vicksburg."

George's face closed. The wariness slipped away, replaced with...nothing. "Miss Althea, I'm doin' just fine."

Althea fingered the intricate latticework on the cast iron bench. *Be my friend*, she wanted to say. *I'm so lonely.* Sometimes the missing of it all, of the years before the war, got so great she thought it might swell up in her chest and burst. Burst just like a mortar shell. Let's go fishing tomorrow, she wanted to say. You bring bait, and I'll talk Flora into wrapping some blackberry cobbler in waxed paper for us to nibble. You and me and Jamie, and maybe we can still tease Franklin into coming too...

But they weren't eight years old anymore. Winston Farm was a blackened ruin, Franklin was serving in the Confederate Army, and Jamie was fighting against them. And she could never be George's friend, and he knew it.

"I'm glad you're thinking about a vegetable garden," she said. "I know we'll all be grateful for that." Then she left him scrabbling in the soil, and went inside.

— CHAPTER 9 —

The Louisiana Bayou Expeditions, March–April 1863

Jamie

In March, the 14th Wisconsin Regiment received orders to guard some army engineers on their way to examine a stretch of the completed canal. The entire path—fifteen miles—lay through a swamp. The engineers traveled by canoe. The Wisconsin boys waded. Sometimes they slogged along within spitting distance of dry land, the banks twined with a disagreeable barricade of entwined willows, briers, thorns, vines, and live oak. When the water rose above their waists, they chopped down enormous cypress trees, dragged them across the deep spot, and sidled across on the trunks.

"I have come to the conclusion," Elisha grunted that afternoon, "that Hell is not a hot place of eternal flames. Hell is wet."

"Your opinion has merit," Ed Houghton muttered. "What do you think, Jamie?"

Jamie paused, struggling to keep his balance while groping for a safe spot to place his foot. The dark water was too thick for him to see the muck they were wading through.

"Don't mind him," Elisha said to Ed. "He's just about quit talking altogether."

"I was feeling for a foothold," Jamie protested.

Elisha shrugged. Jamie stared down at the blackwater. It was odd...he dreaded silence, but he wanted his pards to do the talking and arguing and singing—whatever it took to fill the quiet, and keep unwanted echoes away. He couldn't carry a conversation in a haversack, these days. He wasn't fit to join in the jokes and storytelling at night. A straight-on question often left him struggling to scrape up words, as if English was no longer his native tongue. He missed the old Jamie. It hadn't occurred to him that maybe his friends did too.

A tiny, grim smile twitched at his mouth. The joke was on him: he'd been feeling like a hollow shell—a ghost of his old self—but every minute of this swamp trudge pinched him like a mortal being. His heavy wool trousers, soaked through, weighed as much as three full feed sacks. The briers and canebrake lining their path leaned out to scratch any bit of unprotected flesh. His arms ached from trying to keep his rifle dry. Clouds of gnats hovered around his head. He was tired from trying to keep up with the taller men, and worried about snakes.

And the thought of drawing picket duty that night, here in this swamp, made his blood run like snowmelt in a Wisconsin creek.

The sun was starting to sink, staining the sky with pink and orange, before they landed at a plantation. "Like an island in a flood," Elisha observed as they scrambled

March through the Swamp

"We marched for camp around 8 O. A.M.," noted James M. Tyler of Company E, 14th Wisconsin, "and after running through water and mud & climbing through cane break and getting thoroughly wet with rain we got in to camp just about noon hungry enough to eat a dog." Colin Miller of Company C wrote, "The object of this move is to cut a canal...the engineers pronounce the plan feasable....At the risk of being thought presumptuous I will say that I have grave doubts of the success of the enterprise."

Marching to Victory, 1889, engraving by Leslie, Author's Collection

up a rise onto solid ground. Gum and cottonwood trees flanked the landing area. Aside from an egret they startled into flight, and a half-submerged rowboat tied forlornly to a sycamore, the place looked deserted.

Sergeant Neverman assigned Jamie and Elisha not to picket duty, but to a foraging party. "Let's head up to the plantation," he said. "See what we can find. The boys deserve a decent supper."

Jamie swallowed hard. Stealing food from civilians? Almost as bad as night picket duty! Please God, he prayed silently, don't let there be any women left here—

"Let's go!" Sergeant Neverman shouted.

Jamie's skin prickled as the squad cut across the empty cotton fields. He gripped his gun harder, eyeing the trees lining the fields, but any watchers remained hidden. He pictured the slaves who had chopped cotton under a broiling sun, and picked cotton along the endless, back-breaking rows, pulling sacks and baskets along behind them. The fields were stubbled now, untended, but he imagined he saw the slaves' ghosts among the shadows.

The plantation house was long and low, the back verandah framed by a row of graceful columns. One window had been broken, and a red velvet curtain trailed outside like a wound. A tangle of Virginia creeper, poison ivy, and cowslip vines seemed determined to claim the home. A skeletal hound yipped once as the soldiers approached, then slunk away.

"Hallo the house!" Sergeant Neverman yelled. A chorus of frogs and insects stilled momentarily, then began again. "All right, the place looks deserted," the sergeant said. "Let's go in and see what we can find. Keep your guard up, boys. And I need a couple of you to check the barns and smokehouse."

"I'll go," Jamie volunteered quickly. He didn't want to go inside.

"Me too," Elisha echoed.

Elisha and Jamie didn't find anything useful until they startled a scrawny chicken roosting on top of an abandoned buggy. "A hen!" Elisha breathed, but the chicken evaded his grasp and disappeared into the evening. Elisha's mouth worked. "She can't get far," he announced, and followed like a hunting dog on scent.

"I'll check the smokehouse." Jamie turned a corner, still clutching his gun tightly. Daylight was fading, and he didn't fancy straying too far from his pards. Who had carved this plantation from the inhospitable landscape? Where had they gone?

Although the iron hooks dangled empty, the smokehouse still smelled of smoked ham. Jamie paused, sucking in the aroma. His own smokehouse back in Alma smelled just like this. Every year he had helped his pa tend the low hickory fire, and helped his ma stuff the slippery sausage casings. What he wouldn't give...

Well. Jamie sighed, then turned around. "Elish—"

The word died in his throat as he confronted the man waiting behind him. His skin was very black. He was barefoot and shirtless, and towered over Jamie.

"You one o' Massa Lincoln's sodjers?" the man asked, very softly. Jamie noticed that he held a plaited straw hat respectfully in his hands. Jamie's thudding heart eased back toward normal.

"Uh, yes. Yes, I am."

"My wife, she's needin' help. She's sickly."

Jamie strained to make out the low words. The man's dialect was thicker than he was used to. "Where's everyone else?"

"Family done left when you Lincoln sodjers come. Massa marched most of his best bucks off to Texas first. I'se been hid in de bayou 'cause my wife so sick. The rest, they just run off."

"Let me get my sergeant," Jamie said. "He'll know what to do—"

"No suh." The man shifted his weight, and Jamie caught the ripple of powerful muscles. "We doan need a whole passel of fellas. One of you boys already done hurt my wife. A week or so back. Grabbed her, and hurt her bad. I'se jus' needin' some food. Whatever you got to spare. You're so small, I figure I talk to you."

Jamie shrugged helplessly. "But I don't have any food with me. We're here looking for food ourselves. I've got hardtack and some saltpork back at camp, and coffee. Down by the dock."

"You come back later, and bring me some?"

"No! That is, I can't, I got to talk to my sergeant. Look, why don't you just come with me—"

"I said, I ain't comin' nowhere. I'se just askin' for a bit o' help. If you could just see fit to come back later..."

Later. The gloom of twilight was already descending, stretching shadows across the murky water and stilling the calls of unseen birds. "I can't help you!" Jamie cried, and bolted—smack into Elisha.

"What's the matter?" Elisha asked. The dead chicken dangled from one hand.

"Nothing—that is, there was this slave. Runaway. Former slave, I mean." Jamie already felt like a fool. The sweat cooled on his skin as he led Elisha back around the corner of the smokehouse.

The man was gone. Jamie scanned the undergrowth beyond the clearing. Not a leaf stirred.

"What'd he want?" Elisha asked.

"Help. Food."

Elisha shrugged. "Not much we could do, out here. I don't expect he'd want to tramp back through the bayou with us tomorrow."

"I guess not." A growing horde of liberated slaves—contrabands, the boys called them—had been following the Union Army as they moved through the South. Field hands, old women, young mothers toting babies...the army couldn't feed them, or provide shelter. Even if Sergeant Neverman had come, he probably wouldn't have been able to offer the black man much assistance.

Still, Jamie's heart felt like lead. He had panicked. The thought of traipsing back to this ghostly plantation in the middle of the bayou, after dark, had summoned his nightmares. If only the man had been willing to come meet the sergeant! If only he'd picked someone else to ask for help...

None of the boys slept well that night. The foraging expedition didn't turn up any more than Elisha's chicken, Ed Houghton almost stepped on a rattlesnake while relieving himself, and something thrashed and splashed in the bayou beyond the landing long after dark. But when the first pink flush of dawn prompted the swamp birds' morning serenade Jamie was still awake, thinking about the unseen black woman he'd been too afraid to help.

An untidy collection of men and boys comprised the 14th Wisconsin Regiment: woodcutters who supplied the steamships stopping at Alma, lumberjacks from the northern pine forests, farmboys like Jamie and Elisha, a smattering of former store clerks and teachers and blacksmiths. The roster showed Swissers and Germans, transplanted New Englanders, a handful of Oneida Indians, and a stray Irishman or two. The nine hundred-odd men who'd left Wisconsin had been whittled down to two hundred and fifty, and their shared experiences forged strong bonds.

They also united in marvel of April's weather. As the thermometer edged toward 90 degrees, trees leafed out and blackberry bushes blossomed. "I bet Pa's just tapping his maples for syrup," Elisha said one evening, as he and Jamie lay on their blankets in the tiny tent. "We had a foot of snow on the ground last time I went sugaring with him."

"I wish I was home sugarin' now," Jamie said, but Elisha was already starting to snore.

Although still in Louisiana, the 14th wasn't camped far from the Mississippi River. Jamie let his thoughts drift up that mighty river, all the way to Alma, Wisconsin. Sometimes, remembering that little riverside town, and his own family's farm a few miles out, helped him go to sleep. Had Pa gotten the winter wheat in without his help? Did Mama still stew chicken and dumplings whenever Preacher came for Sunday dinner? Did Pa still scold Mama for lighting too many candles when she darned socks in the evening, and she him for tracking snow inside after chores?

But tonight, against his will, his thoughts drifted determinedly south like a stick in the river's current. He remembered steaming down the Mississippi River with his mother each spring, bound for Vicksburg, where they would disembark and make the short trip to Aunt Clarice's home. That home was gone, now. Burned to the ground. Althea and her sisters had sought shelter in Vicksburg...

And with summer here, General Grant would surely press even harder to take Vicksburg. The general's canal schemes had all failed. But somehow he would get his army to Vicksburg. That certainty buzzed in Jamie's mind. He'd worked hard to shove that knowledge aside all winter, as they slogged through bayous and dug canals and worked like oxen to haul cypress logs clear. Now—

Jamie sat bolt upright as the ground trembled beneath him, bumping his head on the damp canvas. A distant boom of thunder shuddered through the night. "Elisha!" he hissed, as the thunder continued, on and on, an endless roll that dwarfed even the fiercest storm.

Elisha didn't stir but soon Jamie heard voices outside. He crawled into a magnolia-scented night and joined several of his pards.

Ed Houghton lay on his belly, blowing the embers of a cookfire back to life. "That's the heaviest firing I've heard yet," he said, when he was satisfied with the new blaze.

"Where do you think it is?" Jamie asked. He shoved a stick eagerly into the flames.

"Vicksburg," Cyrus Creighton said.

"Surely not!" Jamie protested. "We're a good thirty miles from Vicksburg."

"Nope. That's Vicksburg," Ed agreed. "Anybody got any coffee left?"

Jamie tossed over a dirty little sack of coffee beans, not caring if it was his last bit. He sat on the quivering earth, listening to the rumble of artillery. He felt more tired than he could remember. Had Althea thought more about the warning he'd given her last fall, and traveled north? Were she and her sisters safe? His mother's last letter hadn't mentioned her nieces. But his mother's last letter was six weeks old.

He had no way of knowing where Althea was. He only knew one thing with certainty: The Union Army's final push to Vicksburg had commenced.

— CHAPTER 10 —
Vicksburg, April–May 1863

Althea

Althea snapped to a sitting position in bed as the first thunderous boom of artillery shook the night. "Althea!" Nannie cried, coming awake beside her. "Should we go to the cave?"

"Wait a minute." Althea detached her clinging younger sister, clawed away the mosquito netting, groped for her robe, and shoved her feet into slippers. She fumbled to light a candle and secure it in a lantern.

"Grab your shawl," she shouted to Nannie, struggling to be heard over the ongoing barrage. "I'll go see what's happening."

Althea found Mr. Greenlee on the upper verandah, staring down the hill at the Mississippi River. "Oh my," Althea gasped. Enormous fires burned on the far shore, casting a channel of glimmering light on the river. Several huge black masses were floating down on the current. Every few moments one belched fire, and a few seconds later the cannon's report reached her ears. Shells exploded in the upper part of town. From the street below came frantic shouts as officers scrambled to duty, the clip of galloping hooves as couriers raced away, a woman's distant shriek.

"It's the Yankees," Mr. Greenlee shouted unnecessarily.

Althea gripped the railing, which was quivering with the intensity of the shelling. They'd been able to see the Yankee transport ships for weeks, anchored in the distance north of town and out of range of the Confederate artillery batteries. The Yankees, evidently, had gotten tired of waiting.

"What's burning over there?" she yelled.

"Houses, I think," he shouted back. "Some of our men must have managed to row across the river and start the fires to give our gunners light to see by."

One of the Yankee ships slid in front of the huge fires, and the Confederates' artillery batteries let loose on the brilliantly lit target. Althea clapped her hands over her ears but she could still hear the Confederate cannons' roar, and the horrid scream and boom of Yankee shells approaching and exploding in the air nearby. *Stop it!* she yelled, and felt a bit better.

Mr. Greenlee, however, looked alarmed by her outburst. "My dear, you should get to safety," he yelled in her ear, tugging her arm. "And the other ladies too."

"I'll take them," Althea hollered. "I'm fine. Really." Still, she lingered for one last look at a night on fire. Even up here the glare was bright enough to cast light on the white magnolias and pink crape myrtles framing the balcony, and show the railing's wrought-iron vines and grapes in sharp detail. Confederate soldiers had lighted barrels of pitch on the Vicksburg side of the Mississippi River to help illuminate the water. She could just make out the tiny figures of Confederate sharpshooters on the wharves below, aiming at the boat's crew.

Was Jamie on that ship?

She sent a hasty prayer to the Heavens, asking for his safety, then watched as that Yankee gunboat slid into darkness and another entered the strip of river lit up by the bonfires. "You'll never take us, Cousin," she whispered, and went inside.

A shell burst nearby as Althea, Caroline, Nannie, Mrs. Greenlee, and George hurried out the back door. The Greenlees had hired a digger to provide a cave in the steep bank beside the house. Stump-and-board seats lined the damp, room-sized shelter. Althea set the lantern on the ground and they settled down to wait out the bombardment. "Oh, I do hope there aren't any snakes in here," Mrs. Greenlee fretted. She wore her nightgown and robe and her best blue bonnet.

"I'll check, Miz Greenlee," George offered. He made a careful survey. "No ma'am, none of them critters in here."

Althea watched George as he crouched near the mouth of the cave, where he could watch the shells streak past. Not for the first time, she wondered what he was thinking. She opened her mouth, then closed it again.

Before the Yankees burned their house down, it had never occurred to her to wonder what it felt like to have nothing to call her own. As their three slaves had almost nothing to call their own. But now she knew all too well. She knew what it felt like to rely on others for food, and clothing, and shelter. When the time was

***Admiral Porter's Flotilla Running Past the Batteries of
Vicksburg, Miss., on the Night of the 16th April, 1863***

Confederates lit fires on both sides of the river to help their gunners
target the Yankee ships. One Yankee soldier said, "It was as if hell
itself were loose that night on the Mississippi River."

Author's Collection

right, when this trouble was past, she would find a way
to talk to George. To make it right. Tonight, amidst
the deafening thunder of artillery, was not the time.

Caroline started to sniffle. "Franklin's somewhere
out there," she murmured, wiping away a tear.

Mrs. Greenlee put an arm around her shoulders.
"There, there, dear."

Althea sighed. Comforting words wouldn't calm
Caroline. Caroline would flitter and sniff and watch the
road until Franklin managed to stop by. Now that the
Yankees were kicking up such a fuss, no telling when
that would be.

"Althea, I lost a slipper." Nannie displayed one thin
white foot.

"Come snuggle with me," Althea suggested, and when Nannie had curled on her lap, Althea carefully tucked the hem of her sister's nightdress around the immodest toes. We need to bring more provisions down here, Althea thought. Jars of water. A few blankets. Now that the Yankees were...what? What were they up to this time?

The Greenlees and the three sisters were all in the little formal parlor when Franklin arrived the next afternoon. Caroline was helping Mrs. Greenlee pack away her chandelier so it wouldn't be damaged during this new round of Yankee shelling, and Franklin barely took time to greet his wife before pulling a piece of paper from his pocket. "I need you to hear something," he said, and began to read. "'All noncombatants, especially the women and children, should forthwith leave the city. Heretofore I have merely requested that it should be done; now I demand it.'" Franklin put the notice on the marble-topped table. "That was issued by General Pemberton this afternoon."

Althea put down the book she'd been reading to Nannie and stared at him, trying to wrap her brain around his announcement. General Pemberton was in charge of Confederate defenses in all Mississippi. If *he* was truly ordering them to leave—

"But where would we go?" Caroline cried. The chandelier's crystal teardrops chimed faintly when her hand began to tremble.

A fair question, Althea thought. They'd discussed evacuation before, when the Yankees threatened from one direction or another, without finding a good answer.

"What do you know?" Mr. Greenlee asked quietly.

"Well, as you saw, those Yankee boats tried to slip by our defenses in the dead of night." Franklin paced the parlor. His boots left bits of dried mud on Mrs. Greenlee's clean floor. Neither Mrs. Greenlee nor Caroline scolded him for it, which was the scariest thing that had happened yet.

"We burned one Yankee transport ship and a couple of barges, but most made it past." Franklin smacked one fist against his thigh. "That means all the Yankee soldiers trapped in Louisiana can be ferried across the Mississippi River just south of Vicksburg, where they can attack from a new direction."

"They can't reach Vicksburg," Caroline exclaimed. "They've been trying for almost a year. Vicksburg can't be taken. Our troops will protect us."

"My dear...I'm afraid we'll be facing a bigger assault force than ever before," Franklin told her.

"What about reinforcements?" Mr. Greenlee asked. "Surely the Confederacy will send help. We can't allow Vicksburg to fall!"

"Reinforcements are a possibility," Franklin allowed. "But we have no way of knowing what will happen."

Mrs. Greenlee bobbed her head forward. "I think we should heed General Pemberton's warning, and leave," she dared, then shrank back into her shell.

Mr. Greenlee slowly filled his pipe with tobacco, tamped it down, and tucked away the pouch. "We have friends in the country who will take us in, just as they did last summer. You would all be welcome."

"And there's my family," Franklin said, looking at Caroline.

"I don't want to leave here," Caroline said slowly, patting some straw into the chandelier crate. "Can't we wait and see what happens?"

"How many Yankees got past?" Althea asked, rif-fling the book's pages in her fingers.

Franklin hesitated, his gaze flicking from Caroline to Mrs. Greenlee to Nannie, who was listening intently. "I don't know," he said finally. "And I don't have time to speculate. I have to report back for duty. You need to decide where to take shelter. I don't know how long the roads will be open."

Althea, listen to me, Jamie had implored her last October. *You've got to get out of here. Travel north. My parents will take you in—*

"Althea? What do you think?" Caroline's mouth puckered.

Althea groped for words. *Tell us what to do!* she wanted to shout at Franklin...yet she understood his reluctance to personally burden the Greenlees with the complete protection of his wife and sisters-in-law. She and Caroline needed to decide for themselves, and for Nannie and George. Should they leave Vicksburg? She'd never been comfortable at Franklin's family's home. And the Greenlees' friends were strangers. Taking charity from friends was hard enough to abide!

"How do we know what we'll find if we go?" she asked. "If we travel into the country, aren't we just as likely to be surrounded by Yankees? Who would pro-tect us then?"

"Franklin, I don't want to leave Vicksburg as long as you're here!" Caroline's voice rose.

"But General Pemberton thinks we should go!" Mrs. Greenlee's voice rose too.

Tears trailed down Caroline's cheeks. "I'm sure we're safer here. *Please*, Franklin. Say we can stay."

Franklin hesitated. "If you stay, and trouble comes, you must meet it with your eyes open. Are you prepared for that?"

"Yes, yes," Caroline assured him immediately, then turned to Althea. "You'll stay with me, won't you? We can stay here with Nannie and George. Please?"

Althea looked from Mr. Greenlee, who had obviously made up his mind to take his wife to the country, to Franklin, who looked about to explode with worry for *his* wife. She thought about Jamie and the Yankees, out there somewhere, perhaps even now marching to Vicksburg. And she thought about all the other times the Yankees had tried to take Vicksburg, and failed.

"Yes," she said, and was rewarded by the relief and gratitude in Caroline's eyes. "We'll stay." Why not? They'd already lost everything once, and survived. They'd survive this too.

When Mr. and Mrs. Greenlee went upstairs to pack, Caroline went to the kitchen out back to tell the cook to prepare a hamper of food. "Maybe the gingerbread's done," Nannie said hopefully, and trailed behind Caroline. Althea stared blindly out the front window. Had they made the right decision?

Franklin dropped into a chair beside her, running a hand through his hair. "Althea," he said in a low tone, "I need to talk to you. Those transport ships—we could soon be looking at maybe thirty or forty thousand Yankee soldiers trying to find a way in to Vicksburg."

Forty thousand. "But...the hills," Althea managed after a moment. "We've got the high ground..."

The ghost of a smile touched Franklin's eyes. "The hills will continue to plague the Yankees. We'll defend

Vicksburg. But Althea, I need you to promise that you'll look after Caroline and Nannie. I...I know it sounds silly to ask. But..." He spread his hands helplessly.

"Of course I will," Althea heard herself say, while her brain cried, What can *I* do? Why are you saying these things? Why aren't you talking to your wife?

"If something happens," he whispered, "get to my parents. They'll always make a home for you."

"But—," Althea began, then swallowed her words as Caroline and Nannie came back.

Within an hour the Greenlees had packed. "I wish you would reconsider," Mrs. Greenlee fretted one last time. "What would your dear mother think of me for abandoning you?"

"You've been nothing but good to us," Althea said, hugging her mother's old friend. "We'll take care of your house for you, the best we can."

Nannie sidled closer to Althea. "We'll be fine," she echoed earnestly, her eyes owl-wide. Althea squeezed Nannie's shoulder in thanks. They waved as the Greenlees and their three servants rattled away in their carriage.

Franklin had to leave too. The sisters stood on the front step as he mounted his horse and, after one last look at Caroline, cantered away. Off to face the Yankees, Althea thought, and fought a sudden wave of panic. Was Jamie on one of those transport ships, right this moment? Were he and his army marching on Vicksburg? Why had she agreed to stay?

"Oh, Franklin," Caroline whispered, although he was long out of sight.

"I wish the Greenlees had stayed with us," Nannie added, with a small sniffle.

"Come along," Althea said. "Let's go see about supper."

The Winston sisters tried to settle into a routine. Caroline and Nannie met with other Vicksburg ladies to sew shirts and make bandages for the Confederate wounded, and when guilt got the best of her, Althea went too. Caroline and Althea cooked the simple meals their limited skill and Franklin's money—all they had to live on—allowed. Franklin was able to visit less and less frequently, and Althea watched Caroline's nerves fray accordingly. By the middle of May, when they heard the distant rumble of artillery that suggested the Yankees were finally approaching Vicksburg, Caroline seemed able to do little but pace the hall. Althea's own nerves were stretched taut, and the constant clicking of Caroline's heels plucked like a finger.

"Why don't you read a book?" Althea snapped at last. "You're driving me to distraction!" She had long since read the few books the Greenlees owned, but she knew Caroline hadn't.

Caroline came to the parlor doorway. "You and your books!" she snapped back. "Do you really think some silly novel could occupy my mind? You don't know what it's like to have a husband out there somewhere, in constant danger, never knowing—" Her eyes welled up with tears.

Althea bit her tongue while she scooped up her patience. "Get your bonnet," she said after a moment. "Nannie, you too. I think we all need to get out of the house. Let's go for a walk."

"Do we dare?" Caroline asked, although she reached for her bonnet.

"The gunboats haven't thrown any shells at us today," Althea said firmly. "That artillery you hear is somewhere east of us. Let's find out what's happening."

They took the dizzyingly long flight of steps to a
commanding rise called Sky Parlor Hill, a favorite gathering place for Vicksburg citizens. Several Confederate soldiers manned a telescope under a little brush
arbor they'd constructed to keep the sun away, and
they often invited visitors to survey the surrounding
countryside. Today knots of people hovered near the
observation post. Several of the gentlemen had brought
binoculars. Another was conferring earnestly with a
courier. The Confederate soldiers defending Vicksburg
admired those civilians who had defied General
Pemberton's order to leave the city, and shared what
general information they had.

"What's the news?" Althea asked one of the soldiers. She liked the jaunty collection of blue jay and
wild canary and cardinal feathers stitched carefully into
his shapeless felt hat.

The boy rubbed his hands on his trousers. "Word
is a battle's going on between the Yankee troops and
our boys at Champion's Hill."

Althea felt a chilly flicker along her backbone.
Champion's Hill was only about twenty miles east of
Vicksburg. The closest fight yet, in a string of engage-
ments that had harried Mississippi ever since General
Grant landed his Yankee troops south of Vicksburg.

Then she glanced quickly at her sisters. Caroline's
cheeks had lost all color. Nannie's shoulders were
hunched. "May I look through your telescope?" Althea
asked the feather-bedecked soldier.

"Surely. Although you can't see Champion's Hill from here."

"I know." All she wanted to do was distract her sisters. Turning her back on the rumble from Champion's Hill, she squinted into the army telescope and trained the glass on the Federal encampment visible across the Mississippi River.

"Look," she exclaimed. "I can see a wagon train bringing supplies to the Yankee gunboats. And on shore...there's a Yankee watching us with a glass."

"Oh, Althea..." Caroline twirled one of Mrs. Greenlee's silk parasols nervously, making the black fringe dance. "Let's go down. If Franklin's able to send me word, it will come to the house. And I don't want to be watched by some horrid Yankee."

"Do you want to look, Nannie?" Althea stepped back. Nannie hesitated, her face drawn. "He can't hurt us," Althea added softly.

"Why do they hate us?" Nannie burst out. "I want the Greenlees to come back. Why don't the Yankees just go away?"

"Well, let's tell them to!" Althea grabbed Nannie's hand and pulled her to the edge of the hill. "Hey, Yankees!" she shouted. "Go away!"

"Althea!" Nannie breathed. Her face held a funny mixture of disapproval and delight.

"Try it!"

"Yankees, go away!" Nannie called tentatively.

"Louder!"

"Yankees, go away!" Nannie bellowed.

Althea returned Nannie's grin as Caroline scurried over. "Althea! Nannie!" Caroline breathed. "Whatever are you doing? Stop that at once! It's disgraceful!"

As they rejoined the group at the observation station Althea noticed the surprise on the soldiers' faces, and several women cast disapproving looks her way. But Nannie looked happier than she had since the Greenlees' departure.

Althea had been seven when Nannie was born, and Nannie had grown up delighting in all of the rituals of Southern girlhood that bored Althea to tears. Seeing the smile in Nannie's eyes now, and knowing that she'd put it there, gave Althea an unexpected warm feeling inside. Caroline's embarrassment was a small price to pay.

All that afternoon, women and old men clustered like toadstools on Vicksburg's street corners. When George and Althea ventured out to the market she saw the worry in their faces, and smelled the tension in the air. "Don't worry," she told George. "Our soldiers will protect Vicksburg."

"Yes, Miss Althea."

Althea glanced sideways at George's impassive black face—a face she had always known. When they were children, George sometimes came fishing with her and Jamie, and brought stalks of sugarcane to suck while they lazed on the banks of the Yazoo. After his father died, George had taken responsibility for all the heavy farm chores on his sturdy shoulders. She had always taken George's service and protection for granted.

But she had always taken having a home of her own for granted too.

"George," she said. "Do you know what the Emancipation Proclamation is?"

"Watch your step there, Miss Althea." George shepherded her around a hole carved by a mortar shell before answering. "Yes, I expect I do."

"Then you know that wherever they go, the Yankee Army is liberating the slaves." She remembered the day the Yankees came to the Winston farm the previous autumn, when one had tried to entice George into running away.

"Yes." George kept his gaze on the ground.

"There are roads open, you know." Althea held her skirt aside as a woman swept past on an officer's arm. Her heart began to pound, the way it did whenever the big guns began to fire mortars and cannonballs at Vicksburg. "You could get through."

They turned the corner onto Washington Street. An empty farm wagon clattered past. A woman wearing mourning dress hurried by. Althea wondered how many more mourning veils would be stitched by the women of Vicksburg before the Yankees gave up. And she waited for George's answer.

"Did you want to go to Benson's market today?" George asked. "Or Lovejoy's?"

"Lovejoy's, I think," Althea murmured. "I heard he had some beef." She let her breath out slowly. She didn't know how to feel.

The distant cannonading began again the next morning as Althea pulled on her gloves for church. "That's louder today," Nannie cried. Althea nodded, trying to keep her face clear. Louder. Closer.

At the Methodist Church, an anxious murmur filled the pews. "Our men were pushed back from Champion's Hill," someone said. "I heard they're fighting today at the Big Black River," someone else muttered. "That's only twelve miles from here."

Then one of their neighbors took the pulpit. "Reverend went out to the battlefield," he told the nervous parishioners. They were clustered on the side of the church that had not yet been damaged by Yankee shells. "He asked me to try and provide some words of comfort." Caroline clutched Althea's hand convulsively during the prayers and Bible readings. *Lord Almighty,* Althea prayed. *Help me get Caroline through this. And Nannie too.*

After church the women gathered at Mrs. Balfour's house to prepare more bandages and lint for the hospitals. Today, no one raised an eyebrow at Althea's uneven stitches, or quietly ripped out one of her hems. She wished someone *would.* Instead they sewed in grim silence.

Just when Althea was sure she would explode into a million pieces if something didn't happen to break the tension, one of the women jumped to her feet. "Oh!" she exclaimed, pointing to the front window. "Look!"

They swarmed to the window in time to see a dusty Confederate soldier limping down the street. Then two more, propping each other up, with bloody bandages tied over wounds. Then a group of stragglers, and another, all looking as if they could barely drag one foot after the other. None carried guns.

Caroline broke first, with Althea on her heels, and the women poured from the front door like rice from a bag. "What is it?" Caroline cried, running down the walk. "What's happened?"

"We're whipped," one of the soldiers answered. His left arm hung in a sling. "And the Yanks are after us."

"But—where are you going?" Mrs. Clarkson gasped.

"We're running!" the same man growled, before plodding on.

"Running!" Caroline took a step backwards, as if slapped.

Nannie grabbed Althea's skirt. "Are the Yankees coming?"

"Shame on you for running!" one of the other women cried, and several others took up the frantic chorus: "Shame on you! Stand your ground! Who will protect us if not you? If you don't turn around, Vicksburg will be lost!"

Althea put her arms around Nannie, staring dumbly at the bloodied, hollow-eyed tatters of her army. *No,* her heart hammered. Vicksburg will *not* be lost.

Then she turned to her hostess. "Mrs. Balfour, where is your cistern? Have you buckets handy?"

"Yes." Mrs. Balfour nodded briskly. "Yes, of course. Ladies! Let's bring these poor boys some water."

Althea hauled water to the street for the defeated soldiers until her shoulders throbbed and her palms were blistered. Mrs. Balfour emptied her kitchen of everything eatable for the weary men. She fed some men in the back gallery, and posted Nannie and another little girl at the gate with trays of sliced bread and preserves. Caroline helped pass mugs around the clusters of soldiers until her courage crumbled. "Althea, what's become of Franklin? How can we find out?" Tears poised delicately on her long lashes.

Althea hesitated, rubbing one hand gingerly. "Let's go home," she said finally. "We can wait for news there. I'll fetch Nannie."

Althea kept a hand clamped on each sister's arm as the three edged toward the Greenlees' house on Monroe Street. Soldiers, and families from Vicksburg's outskirts fleeing into the city, jammed the roads—all in a sea of ambulances, yelling officers riding shrilling horses, siege guns, supply wagons, stray mules. The retreating men drove before them milling herds of sheep, squealing hogs, bawling cattle—any livestock likely to fall into Yankee hands if left behind. Althea's knees trembled with relief when she finally pushed Nannie and Caroline through the front gate.

George came to meet them, and Caroline flew forward. "George! Is there any word from Franklin?"

"No, ma'am."

"Why don't you go lie down," Althea said, as Caroline drooped like a forgotten flower. "I'll let you know if there's a bit of news."

"I think I will," Caroline said faintly. She extended a hand to Nannie, and the two went inside. Althea and George began a new bucket brigade.

At twilight, a faint strain of "Dixie" mingled with the din. Althea put down the bucket she'd been lugging to the street. "What's that, do you suppose?" She rubbed her back.

"That's a army band, Miss Althea." George cocked his head. "Up on Courthouse Hill."

"Maybe they're trying to rally the men." Drums began beating above them, soon echoed from below. Althea felt a spark of hope light inside. "That must be it! See? We're not licked yet."

Caroline had roused by the time fresh troops marched by, passing the battered soldiers now resting beneath trees or lying on porches. "Where are you going?" she cried, hanging over the iron fence.

"Out to the entrenchments!" one of them shouted. These boys stepped lively.

"General Pemberton called us up from reserve," another called.

Caroline clasped her hands. "You'll protect us, won't you? You won't retreat and bring the Yankees behind you?"

"We'll never run!" cried one.

"We won't retreat!" cried another.

"We'd die for you ladies!" added a third, although Althea noticed that his gaze didn't leave Caroline's face. Althea kneaded her aching back as she watched another soldier beg for Caroline's handkerchief, presenting her with a button in return. Caroline's smiles did as much for these boys as her own buckets of water had for the beaten ones. Maybe more. Althea's shoulders slumped.

Then the military band struck up "Bonnie Blue Flag," and Althea straightened up. She wasn't competing with Caroline. What did such silly things matter? They had a war to win.

— CHAPTER 11 —
Outside Vicksburg, May 17-19, 1863

Jamie

The Confederates burned the bridge over the Big Black River when they retreated to Vicksburg. After marching twenty miles that day, the men of the 14th Wisconsin Regiment spent the night helping to build two floating bridges across the river.

Hauling planks and timber by the weird light of flickering torches, feeling exhaustion pull at his muscles and weight his eyelids, Jamie stumbled through the night as if in a dream. "I guess I could keep up with the threshing ring well enough if I went back home tomorrow," he muttered to Elisha.

"Hunh," Elisha grunted back. "Your pa can sell his oxen, and use you and me for the pulling."

The next afternoon a military band played "Rally 'Round the Flag" as the 14th Wisconsin marched across the new bridge and on toward Vicksburg. Long lines of infantry wound their way up the hills ahead of them, with flags rippling in a rare breeze. "Huzzah! Huzzah!" the boys yelled, their fatigue vanishing in the excitement of finally, *finally*, moving within spitting distance of their goal. Jamie stared at the blue uniform coat in front of him, trying mightily not to lose the meager bite of roasted salt pork he'd eaten for breakfast. He'd been dreading this return to Vicksburg, but he hadn't known that his first glimpse of that familiar fortress city on the bluffs would hit him like a mule kick in the belly.

The boys' chatter faded as they navigated the uneven terrain. "Looks to me like the good Lord had some bits and pieces left over when he made Mississippi," Elisha panted. "And he flung 'em all down along the river." Gullies and ravines wrinkled the landscape in every direction.

They halted within range of the Confederate fortifications ringing the city. Officers left the 14th standing for an eternity in a light rain while they, evidently, tried to figure out what to do next. Elisha fixed his bayonet on his rifle, rammed the bayonet into the ground in front of him, propped his chin on the up-ended shoulder piece, and promptly went to sleep. "Thanks for the company," Jamie muttered, but it was hard to be irritated by an ability he so longed to cultivate.

Don't think, he ordered himself. *Don't remember.* Don't remember that night in the fog. Don't remember the happier days he'd known in Vicksburg as a boy. He tried instead to survey the landscape as a soldier.

The Union Army faced a seven-mile line of defensive entrenchments. Confederate soldiers had prepared the defense works in a loop around Vicksburg, anchored at each end on the Mississippi River. They held the heights, and could fire down the steep slopes from behind log bulwarks. But Jamie's friends were eager. "They're whipped," Ed Houghton said, squinting at the defensive line. "We should be able to take Vicksburg nice and quick."

When the officers finally told them to make camp, most of the boys rolled up in their blankets and oil-cloths where they stood, too tired for any more elaborate preparations. Jamie lit a candle and reread his mother's latest letter. She sounded lonely. If he could somehow just get his cousins north to Wisconsin, he'd accomplish *something* good. He clung to that hope with both hands. Maybe, he thought, maybe Althea did finally take my advice, and get out of Vicksburg. With that comforting thought, he finally dropped to sleep.

The next morning, officers threw the Wisconsin boys forward in an assault upon one of the Confederate strongholds. Nice and quick, Jamie intoned to himself as he moved forward in a sea of blue. Nice and quick. Dear God, I don't want to let down my pards. I don't want to be a coward. I don't want to fight Franklin. Please let it be nice and quick.

The Confederates, however, had stiffened their backbones since their rout at the Big Black. The 14th advanced up a ravine strewn with stumps and under-brush and cut trees the Confederates had left littering the slope. The tidy shoulder-to-shoulder ranks Jamie so relied on disappeared. The Confederates met the attack with a howling blizzard of lead. Men stumbled and fell, silently or screaming.

Smoke burned Jamie's lungs. He saw Captain Johnson shouting, but couldn't hear his command over the fury of musketry and squealing horses and bellow-ing men. The flag, where was the flag? Jamie couldn't see it. Cyrus Creighton fell with a howl, almost knock-ing Jamie off his feet. *Forward.* Just go forward. Jamie heard himself whimpering as he scrabbled up a steep slope, gasping for breath. He negotiated a gap and finally fell behind one of the fallen trees. Franklin— what if Franklin was up there—

"Jamie!" Elisha appeared in the haze of gunsmoke, a hand over his eyes as if the bullets spitting down the hill were raindrops. "Are you hit?"

"No," Jamie managed, but Elisha wrenched his dirty kerchief free and began fussing with Jamie's right leg. Jamie was astonished to see blood flowing from be-neath his trouser leg, over his ankle. He couldn't re-member being hit. Didn't feel any pain. But he let Elisha shove him back toward the Union lines.

— CHAPTER 12 —
Vicksburg, May 19, 1863

Althea

"I just don't know what to do," Caroline said, walking back across the parlor. The sandalwood fan in her hand quivered back and forth with admirable speed. "I hate the thought of going out."

"Then stay home." Althea made a knot and bit the thread, then surveyed her seam. Definitely crooked. She was making a tiny sewing kit, called a "housewife," to give to some Confederate soldier in need.

"But if I stay home, the other ladies will think I'm not doing my part."

Althea stifled a sigh as she tugged on the housewife, trying to straighten the seam. "Then go."

Caroline perched on the edge of a chair. "Althea...do you suppose it's too late to leave Vicksburg?"

"What?"

Caroline jumped back to her feet. "Well, the fighting is horrible, and so close...I'm thinking about Nannie, really. Perhaps we should have gone with the Greenlees."

Althea blew out her breath slowly before answering. "There's a ring of Yankees out there. Vicksburg is surrounded. It's really too late to have this conversation."

Click, click, click. Caroline needed exactly nine paces to cross the room. Nine back.

Althea tried again. "Caroline, you have too much time on your hands. Why don't you go to the hospital? That request for help sounded desperate."

"But I'm just not sure—"

"Oh, for Heaven's sake, Caroline! You're dithering like a goose!" Althea dropped the misshapen housewife on the table. "And you're giving me a headache."

Two tiny spots of indignant color appeared in Caroline's cheeks. "Well! It's easy for you to judge. *You're* not a married lady. You're not the one responsible for Nannie. And you weren't asked to go to the hospital."

Althea shoved to her feet. "No, but perhaps I should go anyway."

Caroline's jaw dropped. "You can't! It's not seemly for unmarried girls to tend soldiers."

Althea clenched her hands in the folds of her skirt. "Maybe what's seemly should be reconsidered, under the circumstances." The more she thought about it, the more she liked the idea. *Anything* was better than spending one more moment cooped up with Caroline through another endless afternoon, waiting for news that never seemed to come. They knew only that more fighting was underway around Vicksburg's defensive line—closer than ever.

She tossed the housewife to Caroline. "Here—we'll trade. You finish this, and I'll go to the hospital in your place." She headed for the walnut hall tree, where her bonnet and shawl waited.

"Althea Winston! Don't you dare!" Caroline cried, but Althea was already out the door. She slammed it with a bit more force than necessary and headed down the walk.

Guilt poked her as she made her way down Monroe Street. A shell from one of the Yankee gunboats whistled overhead and exploded several blocks away. She briefly considered going back, but couldn't bring herself to do it. She'd been caged up too long already! It was about time she found something useful to do. Caroline and Nannie could stitch the silly housewives, and take it upon themselves to scoot to the cave if the shells started falling any closer. And George was there—he wouldn't let any harm come to her sisters.

Althea's steps quickened as she made her way to the City Hospital. In addition to the gunboats tossing mortar shells into the city, the Yankees fired long-range rifles from the Louisiana side of the river. They had also parked several big guns, which the men called "Parrott guns," behind the levees over there. The Parrott guns sent whirring, cone-shaped missiles that could be heard well before striking. Althea feared the rifles the most. She knew that by the time she heard the *ziiip* of a rifle ball, it was too late to hide.

I won't cower underground if I can be useful, she thought, setting her jaw. There were two kinds of hospitals in the city, one for sick soldiers, and one for wounded. Many of the Vicksburg wives routinely spent time in them, and Caroline had several times visited sick soldiers during the winter months. But ambulances had brought hundreds of bleeding soldiers into town

The Shell, by Howard Pyle, 1908

Emma Balfour noted, "In some parts of town, the streets are literally ploughed up. Many narrow escapes have been made..." Hosea Rood of the 12th Wisconsin reported that a comrade using binoculars saw "a lady walking down a street and leading a little girl. A shell, or piece of one, struck the child killing her instantly. Poor people!"

after the recent battles, and today's fighting would certainly send more. The hospitals were overflowing, and desperate hospital matrons had sent errand boys with pleas for help.

"And shame on them if they send me away," Althea muttered. Her lips twitched in a grim smile as she imagined herself pleading with some formidable nurse: "Please, ma'am, let me stay. If I have to spend one more minute watching my sister flutter and wring her hands I'll go absolutely mad."

Her resolve carried her down the torn up pavements to the City Hospital. Rows of clotheslines sagging with bed linens flanked the three-story building. Confederate soldiers sat at the windows, and lay on the grass outside. A newsboy picked his way among them, selling papers. A man hobbled by on crutches. Ambulances and farm wagons and buggies and carriages lined the street in front—all, Althea realized, carrying more wounded soldiers. Her steps slowed as she watched two men lift a litter from a wagon. The man lying on it was a blur of homespun and blood. Blood dripped from the litter as they carried it inside. Althea closed her eyes for a moment, pressing a hand against her mouth. She wished she'd brought George along.

After steadying her nerves she hurried up the steps. Inside the hall a new barrage hit her: the smell of blood, the sight of more bloodied men—some missing arms, or legs—lying in neat rows along the corridor, and the chorus of groans from the rooms beyond. Someone was crying for his mother. An older voice yelled "No, no, no," on and on and on. A sickly smell lingered in the hall. Althea pressed a hand against the wall, trying to draw strength from the cool plaster.

She wished she'd listened to Caroline.

Then a woman hurried toward her. Mrs....Mrs. Martin, wasn't it? Althea remembered her from the sewing circle. Then, she was dressed in a lovely lavender dress blossoming over an enormous hoop skirt. Today she wore serviceable brown cotton over a small corded petticoat, hemmed to the ankle.

"Have you come to help?" Mrs. Martin asked. She rubbed her temples with bloodstained hands. Blood caked under her fingernails formed dark little crescents. "Bless you, child."

Althea wet her lips. "I guess so...that is, I don't really know anything about nursing—"

"It doesn't matter." Mrs. Martin propelled her by the elbow toward an open doorway. "We'll keep you away from the surgeons, but there's plenty of work to do." She faced Althea toward the ward. "Be useful."

"But—," Althea began, but Mrs. Martin was already gone. Althea faced a ward crammed with cots, each occupied by a broken man. Most were covered with blankets or sheets, although a few lay only in the rags of their uniforms. Althea's frantic gaze took in missing arms. Missing legs. Bloody bandages. Buzzing flies. Crusted wounds. The room smelled of blood and chamber pots.

She stood frozen until she finally realized that the man nearest her was trying to get her attention. "Miss," he croaked. "Miss."

"Um...yes?" Althea edged to his cot. He was young—no older than Franklin—with ginger hair plastered to his head with sweat, and a surprising smattering of freckles. His hands flicked convulsively at the sheet. Althea licked her lips again, feeling sick. She

had seen wounded soldiers, of course—discharged veterans hobbling down the street, a few officers with
empty sleeves pinned neatly up. But not like this. Not
looking to her to *help* them.

His eyes were full of pain. "Could you get me some
water...please?"

Oh. Oh, thank the Lord. This she could do. "Of
course," she whispered. As she looked around for a
pitcher or bucket, she let her fingers lightly touch the
boy's forehead. It was hot and damp. *This boy might
die*, she thought, and almost jerked her hand away.
But then she saw his lips curl toward a smile, and his
eyes drift closed, and she let it stay.

"Are you living underground?" the man with no legs
asked, several hours later. He was older than most of
the others, with a liberal sprinkling of gray in his dark
hair.

Althea managed a smile. "Not quite. We have a
little cave we run to when the shelling starts, but we're
trying to stay in our house. There are some big caves
nearby, though. Some are quite elaborate, I'm told."

"You shouldn't be here, miss," a younger man on
the next cot fretted. "Vicksburg is no place for women
and children."

"We had the chance to get out," Althea said softly.
"We chose to stay. We trust our army to defend
Vicksburg. The Yankees will *never* take Vicksburg."

"God bless the women," the older man murmured.

Althea closed his hand around one of the leafy
walnut branches she'd gathered. "Here. Can you hold
on to this? Use it to help keep the flies away. Did you
get enough water for now?... Good. Try to rest, then."

She was about to move on when she noticed Mrs. Martin beckoning from the doorway. Smudges of exhaustion ringed the older woman's eyes. But as Althea approached, that beautiful sweet smile erased the fatigue lines around Mrs. Martin's mouth. "You're still here?" Mrs. Martin murmured. "I'm going home to get some sleep. You should come too, dear."

Althea looked back over the ward, opened her mouth to protest, then realized how bone-weary she was. "Well...all right. I'll come back later."

"That's fine." Mrs. Martin shepherded Althea to the front door. "Just remember, you'll be no good to these men if you let yourself get worn down."

Darkness had slipped over Vicksburg. As Althea and Mrs. Martin stepped outside, a Yankee gunboat launched a mortar shell. Althea watched it arc through the sky like a shooting star, decided it would go safely overhead, and went on down the steps. "I'm not worn down," she murmured, although she wasn't sure if Mrs. Martin heard over the screaming whine of the approaching bomb. "I've never felt better."

— CHAPTER 13 —
Outside Vicksburg, May 22–23, 1863

Jamie

General Grant decided to launch one final assault. The attack was sudden and complete. Every Union artillery battery along the entire line began with a prolonged barrage. Sharpshooters sniped at the Confederate defenders at the same time, and gunboats on the Mississippi let loose at Vicksburg too. Only after two hours of this earth-shuddering, deafening offensive did the infantry soldiers rush forward, bayonets glinting in the sun.

Jamie's calf wound wasn't serious, but it had bled profusely and now hurt like anything, and Captain Johnson ordered him to stay behind. Jamie couldn't find the energy to protest, and could only hope his pards didn't brand him a coward. They didn't seem to; instead they quietly handed him letters, watches, and tintypes of mothers and sweethearts, and asked him to "take care of things" if they didn't return from the attack.

Jamie sat under a pine tree behind the Union lines and listened to the assault, snapping dead pine needles

111

into tiny pieces. Waiting, that was always worse than anything else. Waiting to learn which pards would be hurt or killed was just as bad, he discovered, as waiting to march into battle himself.

The haze of smoke and tortured terrain prevented Jamie from seeing much of the attack. After an eternity of waiting he saw the first wounded Yankees stumbling back to safety. Then more, and more...and soon the unhurt soldiers too, bitter and dazed, in full retreat.

Jamie crumbled a few more pine needles, then took a deep breath and shoved to his feet. He crested a small rise and paused beneath a tree, looking for his pards. His hands clenched, wondering who still lay on the field.

A group of mounted officers trotting down the line paused near Jamie's tree. One used a pair of field glasses to survey the torn landscape. Another, a stocky dark-haired man with a cigar clamped between his teeth, pulled a piece of wood from his pocket and began to whittle.

A civilian riding with them—a reporter, maybe— leaned toward the dark-haired man. "What's your plan, General Grant? Are you going to try another assault? Or give up on Vicksburg altogether?"

The dust-covered general slowly removed the cigar from his mouth. "Neither," he grunted. "We'll dig our way in." He tossed the sharpened stick on the ground and kneed his horse forward.

The reporter caught the arm of one of the other officers. "And what about the civilians in Vicksburg?" he pressed.

Jamie held his breath. His temples began to throb.

"We'll starve 'em out."

Siege of Vicksburg—Sherman's Attack on the Confederate Works, May 22, 1863, by F.B. Schell

Note the Union soldiers at rest beneath shelters designed to protect them from the sun, while soldiers on the front line fire through their fortifications. The Confederate fortifications are among the trees, and Vicksburg is just visible in the distance.

The group trotted after General Grant. Jamie sat back down abruptly. *Oh, Althea...I pray God you got out.*

The Yankees began digging toward the Rebel defenses. Red-faced, sweating Northern boys fought with shovels and spades, and every day, trenches snaked closer to the Southern lines.

Ninety-seven men of the 14th Wisconsin had been killed or wounded during the final, failed assault on Vicksburg. The rest soon got their taste of this new kind of warfare. They crept into the Union rifle pits before dawn's light. Jamie found that the dirt removed during the digging had been piled on the Confederate side of the trenches, and soldiers had arrayed grain sacks filled with sand on top of that, with two-inch gaps between each bag. Jamie dutifully propped his rifle barrel in a crevice between sand bags, cocked the trigger, poised his finger.

"Shoot at anything that moves," Sergeant Neverman ordered. "And for God's sake, stay down. They've got sharpshooters watching."

This was a new kind of waiting. Gunboats threw mortars at Vicksburg from the Mississippi, and Yankee artillery shelled Vicksburg from behind, and in between explosions Jamie heard the crunch of shovels as other Yankee soldiers worked to advance the trench lines toward the Confederate works. As the hours ticked by, Jamie began to wonder if he might go mad from the incessant thunder of artillery, or from staring at the dead soldiers blackening in the sun between the lines.

"You'd think they'd at least let us bury our dead," Elisha muttered, echoing his thoughts.

"You'd think."

The sun rose higher. Sweat rolled into Jamie's eyes. His hands cramped. His legs ached. Jamie began to wonder if he'd die of sunstroke, or pure thirst. His canteen was long empty. His tongue shriveled in his mouth, and produced no effect when he scraped it along his cracked lips. He spotted a wild plum bush in the dead man's stretch between the lines and stared at a ripe fruit until his vision blurred. That plum was surely the most juicy, sweet, refreshing piece of fruit in all Mississippi. That was a plum worthy of his ma's best jelly. A plum deserving the grand prize at the Agricultural Fair. A plum worth savoring slowly while the juice ran down his chin—

"Hey!" someone shouted. Jamie tore his gaze from the plum and saw an old half-starved mule ambling close to the Yankee lines—just as a hundred muskets exploded. Jamie almost jumped from the trench. The mule dropped, riddled with lead.

"What are you doing?" Jamie hollered, turning on the boys nearest to him in the line. "What is the matter with you?"

"What's the matter with you?" Jacob Clark shot back, ripping a new cartridge open so he could reload.

"Yeah, c'mon, Jamie," Elisha added. "No harm done."

"What do you mean, no harm done?" Jamie glared at his friend. "That mule belonged to someone, you know! Maybe a family in Vicksburg that needed it!"

Elisha and Jacob exchanged long glances. Jamie sank down in the trench. He was trapped here in this hole, while his own army rained fire on a city full of women and children. And his throat was closing shut

Federal Troops in the Entrenchments before Vicksburg,
by McComas

After the Union assaults upon Vicksburg failed, and the officers decided to besiege the city, soldiers dug an elaborate network of trenches.

Author's Collection

from thirst. Maybe he should just go for that plum. Just rise above the entrenchments and march right over to that plum—

"Hey, Jamie." Elisha grabbed his arm, speaking in a low tone. "Jamie!"

"I'm all right."

"The boys were just having some sport, you know? We needed something to break the monotony."

"I know." Jamie scrubbed beads of sweat from his face. "I just keep thinking about all the women and children—"

"It's hard! But Crimus, Jamie, we're fighting a war! If our gunners could just take out the Rebel defenses and never hurt another thing, they would. Civilians had plenty of time to leave Vicksburg. They just stayed out of pure stubbornness. The sooner they give in, the sooner the war will be over."

I know all that! Jamie wanted to holler. But shooting that mule wouldn't help the Union Army's cause.

"Here." Elisha reached for a long forked stick lying in the bottom of the trench, and settled his blue cap on the tip. "Let's have some fun," he said. "All right, boys, what's your wager?"

The boys within earshot stopped staring at Jamie. "Three," Ed Houghton said.

"Seven," someone else called.

Jacob Clark spat on the ground. "Those Rebels? I'd say none!" That brought some hoots and cheers.

"Jamie?" Elisha asked pointedly.

Jamie felt all eyes upon him. He knew that look of Elisha's: *Come on, boy. Participate.* "Uh, eight," Jamie said.

Elisha smiled. "And I say a neat half-dozen." He slowly raised the stick until the cap showed clearly above the log breastwork above their trench. Instantly Jamie heard the whine of Minié balls, and little spitting sounds as they hit the Mississippi clay.

"Whoo-wee!" Elisha let the cap drop, and quickly counted the bullet holes. "Four. That's some poor shooting, I do say. Ed wins that round."

Ed grinned. "What do I win?"

"Our eternal esteem," Elisha said, and the boys laughed. Jamie gave Elisha a grateful glance. I owe you one, he tried to say with his eyes.

No one was more eager than Jamie to see the sun sink toward the horizon. "We'll get recalled soon," someone muttered. Someone else passed a full canteen down the line, and Jamie gulped like a thirsty dog. For the first time in hours, the deafening bombardment ceased. Jamie soaked in the silence, and felt some of his reason return. "I'll cook supper tonight," he told Elisha.

Elisha sighed. "Hope we got some good grub waiting. I figure General Grant knows what he's doing, but if we don't get a supply train up here soon, he's not going to have much of an army left. We can only live off the land for so long—"

"Hey, Jamie!" one of the boys called from down the line. "They're asking for you!"

"Who is?"

"I don't know! Someone further along."

What was that about? Jamie looked at Elisha. "Guess I better go. Tell Sergeant Neverman, will you?"

Engineers had directed that the Union trenches be made in zigzag fashion to provide better protection to the boys digging and defending them. Jamie scrabbled down the line to the newest section. "Who's looking for Jamie Carswell?" he asked several times, and was twice pointed further along the line. Finally he found himself among some Missouri troops.

"You're Jamie Carswell?" one of them asked. Jamie nodded. "Well, you're as close to the Rebel lines as you can get. We found out this afternoon there's some Missouri boys just across the way, in the Rebel lines. We've been catching up on the news."

Jamie nodded again. He knew Missouri had sent troops to both armies. But he hadn't any idea what that had to do with him.

A lanky redhead leaned close to the edge of the trench. "Hey, Joe!" he hollered. "You still there?"

"That you, Seth?" The reply was distant, but clear.

"I got that Wisconsin fellow here!" Seth yelled.

Jamie wiped perspiration away with his sleeve, growing more bewildered. Then a different voice drifted across the dead man's zone between the lines. "Hey, Jamie?"

Jamie clutched at the clay bank. "*Franklin?* Is that you?"

"Sure is!"

Jamie stared at the redhead. He had delivered a miracle. "What are you doing?"

"Defending Vicksburg! What're *you* doing?"

The sun had soaked Jamie's brain. He was desperate to talk to Franklin, and didn't know what to say. "I wish I could see you!" he yelled finally.

"Don't!" Franklin bellowed back, the warning clear in his voice. Jamie remembered Elisha's cap, the instant hail of Minié balls.

Jamie pressed his cheek against the clay bank. "Are you well, Franklin?"

"Well enough. How about you?"

Jamie glanced at the Missouri redhead, who was following the exchange with interest. "Well enough," he managed. Then he screwed up all his courage. "Franklin—what about the girls? Did the girls get out of Vicksburg? Did Althea and Caroline take Nannie to my mother?"

The pause seemed so long Jamie wondered if Franklin had left. Finally, "No. They're still here."

Jamie closed his eyes. Why, *why* hadn't Althea listened to him? That stupid, headstrong girl!

"Jamie?"

"Franklin," Jamie hollered. "Maybe it's not too late. If you can get them out, send them north. Alma, Wisconsin. My folks will take care of them."

"Jamie? I've got to go."

"Give them my regards," Jamie yelled. A ridiculous thing to say. "Tell Althea..." What? What could he tell her?

"Take care of yourself, Jamie!"

"You too, Franklin!"

Boom! The Union artillery blasted a fresh round toward Vicksburg. Jamie slid to the ground, leaning against the trench wall. His rifle slipped from his fingers.

"It's tough, ain't it?" the redhead said sympathetically. "I went to school with some of the fellas over there."

But they joined the Confederate Army, Jamie thought. Like Franklin. It hurts like fire to fight against Franklin, but he and I both chose to become soldiers. Althea and her sisters, and the other women and children in Vicksburg, they hadn't made that choice. For a moment, he considered telling this stranger from Missouri everything bottling up inside.

But the new bombardment was making his head ache. "Yeah, it's tough," he agreed, and left it at that.

— CHAPTER 14 —

Vicksburg, May 25, 1863

Althea

Althea glanced up from the frying pan as George opened the kitchen door. "I found a few things, up on the hill," he said. "Thought they might go good for breakfast." He deposited a double-handful of ripe blackberries on the table like gold. Then he rummaged in his pocket, and pulled out a twisted, orange-tan root.

"Oh, bless you!" Althea breathed. "Blackberries *and* a sassafras root! That will cheer Caroline and Nannie up." Food became more dear with every passing day. The blackberries would go well with the corn cakes she was frying for breakfast, and they hadn't had coffee or tea in weeks. "I think we should venture to the market today, if the shelling doesn't get too bad—"

"Franklin!"

Caroline's scream came from the house. Althea stared at George, the spoon slipping from her fingers and clattering to the floor. "Oh Lord," Althea breathed, thinking, Franklin is dead. Franklin is dead, and Caroline just got the word.

121

Althea snatched up her skirt and bolted across the breezeway and into the house, George on her heels. They found Franklin in the front hall. Dust filmed his gray uniform but he was very much alive. Caroline clung to him. "Oh, Franklin," she quavered. "I've been sick with worry. We knew battles were going on—why didn't you send word?—oh, Franklin..." Just then Nannie clattered down the stairs, threw herself at Franklin, and wound her arms around his legs.

Althea and George exchanged another look before Althea leaned against the wall, weak-kneed with relief. "It's good to see you, Franklin," she managed. "Caroline, you took a year off my life."

"Is your horse outside, suh?" George asked. At Franklin's nod, George slipped outside to tend the mare.

Franklin gently detached his wife, kissed the top of Nannie's head, and eased her aside too. "I didn't have a moment until now," he said. Dark circles rimming his eyes, the slight shake in his hands, lent truth to his words. "But I'm all right. I'm all right."

Still clinging to his hand, streaked now with yellow dust, Caroline smiled. "Althea was making breakfast. We'll get you fed, and you can take a bath—"

"I can't stay," Franklin said, shaking his head. "I have to get back. I just needed to see you. To make sure you're all safe, and let you know that I am too."

"But—oh, I see." Caroline made an effort to control her disappointment. Franklin smoothed her hair, rocking her gently. Althea reached a hand toward Nannie, wanting to give the couple a moment of privacy, but he stopped her: "Althea, wait. I talked to Jamie."

She blinked, and sagged back against the wall. Jamie. Franklin said he'd talked to Jamie. "You *what*?"

"The lines are close enough that some of the boys were hollering back and forth. I managed to have a few words." He shrugged slightly, a tiny smile tugging at his mouth. "Not a very rewarding conversation, but he said he's well. And he asked about you."

Althea plucked at the gold fringe on the table-cloth covering the little round table beside her. Her mind whirled back to the prisoner she'd seen last Oc-tober. "How—"

"I'll explain later. I don't have much time now. But— if I can arrange it, do you want to see him?"

"What?"

"There's going to be a short cease-fire this after-noon." Franklin looked at Althea intently. "It's not with-out some risk, but if you want—"

"I'll do it," Althea said. She'd heard all she needed to hear.

Franklin and Althea rode from Vicksburg to the Confederate defensive line, about two miles from the city. He stopped near a group of officers' big tents, and helped her dismount. The entrance to a small cave yawned in the bank behind her.

"One of the men had this dug for his wife," Franklin said. "It's a good place for you to wait. It may take a while. I don't even know for sure I'll be able to find him. The truce is supposed to hold for another two hours. But at the first sign of trouble, you get inside that cave. Hear?"

"I hear."

"I mean it, Althea." Franklin removed his hat and ran a hand through his hair.

"I'll be fine." Althea settled on a convenient log. It was quiet, for the first time in a week. She couldn't ask for more.

Franklin handed her a pair of field glasses he'd had slung over his shoulder. "You can see what's happening on the field. But do *not* wander any closer. Do you hear me?"

Althea turned on him. "Franklin, would you stop fussing and go already?"

He regarded her with a look of exasperated affection before leaving her alone.

Althea dabbed her forehead with her handkerchief, wishing for shade. Balls or shells had stripped the nearby honey locust trees of most of their foliage. Caroline had insisted Althea bring a parasol, but Althea felt ridiculous sitting on a log above a battlefield with a parasol in hand, and she left it closed. Her bonnet would have to do. Instead she used both hands to focus the field glasses.

Franklin had chosen her perch well. She could see beyond the officers' tents and brush awnings, busy with couriers and cooks and soldiers tending horses, to the Confederate defensive works. She could see the trenches, and the log bastions constructed on the Yankee side of them. And she could see beyond them to the field—

Althea abruptly dropped the field glasses into her lap. She pressed a hand against her mouth. Franklin had explained, of course, that the officers of both armies had agreed to this truce in order to collect and bury the dead left from the failed Yankee assaults on the Confederate lines. She had seen dead soldiers before, in the hospital. That had been bad enough. She hadn't known what dead soldiers looked like after several days on a field beneath the blazing Mississippi sun. Blackened. Bloating.

When she could, she raised the glasses again. Skirting the burial details, she focused instead on the strange bustle of activity along the lines. Men swarmed like ants over both sets of breastworks, the protective fortifications they'd built. She saw Yankees in blue coats, Confederates in gray and butternut, chatting together. In the Confederate lines she saw flasks offered, tobacco pouches traded. A number of Confederates ambled toward the Union lines, where she assumed they would be given as warm a reception. An unexpected lump rose in her throat.

An hour or more passed before she heard Franklin call her name. His hand rested protectively on Jamie's shoulder as they wound through the Confederate bustle behind the lines. Althea rose slowly to her feet. Sure enough. Jamie.

"Hullo, Althea." Jamie shifted his feet awkwardly.

The lump jumped back into her throat. She impulsively threw her arms around her cousin's filthy Yankee coat, then stepped back. "Heavens above, Jamie. You smell just as bad as you did the last time I saw you."

"It's good to see you too, Althea."

He looked somehow both bigger and smaller than she remembered. Taller, maybe, and much more solid through the shoulders and arms. But skinnier. The dark fuzz on his chin was new, too. "You faring well?" she asked.

"Well enough. And you?"

"Well enough—"

"For God's sake, Althea," Jamie exploded. "What are you doing here?"

She folded her arms. "I came to see you, you ninny!"

"No, no, I mean in Vicksburg. Why didn't you get out? I *told* you to get out, I told you!"

Althea frowned. She didn't know what she wanted of this visit, but another argument was surely not it. "And I told you, we're fine where we are."

"Althea, if you could just get to Wisconsin—"

Heavens above, he sounded like Caroline! "It's too late to even have this conversation, Jamie. If you hadn't noticed, your army has surrounded Vicksburg."

"You might still be able to get through—"

Franklin coughed. "Let's sit down," he suggested. Althea settled back on her log. Franklin found a convenient stump, and Jamie sat on the ground. "I told you she wouldn't go for it," Franklin said to his friend.

"And I will never understand why you let them stay."

A muscle worked in Franklin's jaw, and Althea saw a rare flash of anger in his eyes. "Maybe you've been away too long," he said after a moment. "Southern women are the Confederacy's backbone. I won't ship my wife and sisters-in-law north if they don't want to go."

"The roads are all closed anyway," Althea added. "A cat couldn't walk out of Vicksburg, from what I hear."

"But—but you know this country. You could slip through cross-country—"

"Maybe I could, if your sentries didn't shoot me for trying," Althea snapped. "But Caroline and Nannie? I don't think so. I wouldn't leave them even if I wanted to. And you know what? I don't. And I don't want to talk about this anymore!"

Jamie was silent for a long moment. A mule staked nearby brayed shrilly. A distant burst of laughter drifted up the slope. Finally he put a hand on her arm. "Althea," he whispered, "*please*. Do this for me. I...I'm begging you. If I could just get you away safe, if I could just know that, maybe it would make up for...for all the rest."

Something in his eyes, his tone, made the hairs on the back of Althea's neck prickle. She remembered something he'd said last October. *Althea...there was this one night, on guard duty, I got lost in the fog, and...* And what? He hadn't finished the story. But she knew that something terrible had happened to him that night in the fog. Something he still carried.

The question rose on her tongue, but the words simply didn't come. "You're hurting me," Althea said finally, as gently as she could, pulling her arm away from his convulsive grasp.

Jamie's hand dropped. His shoulders slumped. "I'm afraid for you," he whispered.

"You mustn't be. I'm not afraid," she said stoutly. "It's not so bad. Really."

His look bordered on scorn. "Althea, they're *shelling* the city! Oh, they're aiming for the batteries, but I *know* you're getting shelled. And it's only going to get worse."

"The hardest part is getting used to it," Althea said slowly. "Once you do...it's not so bad."

Jamie stared at her, disbelieving. Althea spread her hands. "You must know how it is," she tried. "We're learning. When we hear a shell we watch for it, and listen. Most always they don't come too close. If they do, as long as the shell gets over your head you're safe, because even if it explodes the pieces will fall beyond you. We have a little cave near the house. Nannie doesn't even cry anymore, she just knows to run for the cave if the shells come too close..."

"God Almighty!" Jamie breathed.

Too late, Althea noticed the look of pure horror on Jamie's face. "Don't worry," she ended lamely, feeling like an idiot.

Jamie shook his head. "Althea," he said deliberately. "Franklin...the Union Army is going to take Vicksburg. You both must know it."

"I *don't* know that," Althea blazed. "We're just waiting for reinforcements. They're on their way. Everyone knows it. Once the reinforcements come, you boys'll be sent scrambling back north."

Franklin answered more quietly. "All I know is that we'll defend Vicksburg to the last."

The pain in Franklin's eyes hurt. Althea leaned forward. "Jamie, listen to me. You don't know the spirit of the people in that city. You Yankees will *never* take Vicksburg." Franklin's tired smile rewarded her.

Jamie opened his mouth to argue, but Franklin pulled out his pocketwatch. It hung from a fob woven from Caroline's hair, and he stroked it absently with a finger before tucking it back away. "I think we better head back," he said to Jamie. "I'll guarantee your safety, but it's best if you're back in your lines when the truce officially ends."

"Already?" Althea asked. They'd had so little time— and most of it wasted! She felt tears well up as Jamie scrambled to his feet, and she gave him another fierce embrace. "Don't worry about us," she whispered. "Just take care of yourself."

He nodded, and tried to smile, but it didn't reach his eyes. "Give my love to Caroline and Nannie—oh, wait. I almost forgot." He fumbled with the leather haversack hanging at his side. "I brought you a couple of things. I wish it was more. I didn't have much time. But, here." He extracted a small, very dirty muslin bag, but Althea focused on what came out next.

"A book!" she breathed, snatching it. An orange border framed an enticing woodcut illustration on the cover. "Oh, I have *ached* for a new book! There's so little to do here, especially when the bombardment is heavy." She stroked the battered little volume lovingly. "Beadle's New Dime Novels. *Malaeska, the Indian Wife of the White Hunter*. It looks like a great adventure."

"Somebody brought it back from a foraging trip." Jamie snorted wryly. "The boys will be sore at me for giving it away before they had a chance to read it. But it belongs to you more than us, anyway." He nodded. "Be safe, Althea."

Althea clutched the book to her heart as Franklin and Jamie wound back through the commotion toward his own lines. A book. Jamie had given her a book. For the first time in ever so long—since Papa left home—someone had done something purely to make her happy.

The tears welled up and over again. "Drat," she muttered angrily, wiping them away. She wished she'd had a gift to give Jamie. She wished she'd been able to even say something to make him happy.

"I'll stay safe," she whispered. "And keep Caroline and Nannie safe too. We'll all come through this all right. You'll see." It was the only promise she could think to make.

— CHAPTER 15 —
Outside Vicksburg, June 1863

Jamie

"I would sell my soul," Elisha said, "for a clean shirt."

"At least we got good food tonight!" Ed Houghton said. "Dig in, boys!"

The latest foraging party had brought back armloads of booty: sweet potatoes, a crock of pickled cabbage, smoked ham, dried apples and peaches, even biscuits with butter. "We found a place, looked like the family just ran off without packing a thing," Jacob Clark reported. "A music book open on the piano bench. Biscuits just waiting on the table." He spread butter on a biscuit with a dirty finger, and popped it in his mouth. "Say! This is first rate."

Jamie chewed a dried peach slowly. He knew he needed to eat. The 14th spent only every other day standing watch in the trenches. But they spent a good portion of most nights repairing the damage done during the day's fighting, and extending the trenches closer to the Confederate works. It was the safest time to work, so by moonlight they strengthened torn-down breastworks with heavy timbers and cotton bales, filled and dragged heavy sandbags, carved out new trenches with pickax and spade. Jamie had learned to crawl with his rifle in one hand and a shovel in the other. He also tried to keep a sharp eye on Elisha, who almost got his skull cracked by a swung shovel one night when he fell asleep in the shadows. Jamie didn't want to let his pards down. So he ate.

If only Franklin hadn't looked so thin. Althea too. Neither had mentioned food, and Jamie could only imagine the short rations already plaguing Vicksburg's citizens and defenders. But he hadn't seen either of them in seven months, and the change was startling. If only he'd had the presence of mind to grab more rations, that day of the truce, when Franklin had sent word to meet him. Although...Althea's face had lit up like a candle when he gave her the book. That was surely the nicest moment of the war.

"Poker," Elisha announced, when the meal was through. "We got time before dark. Who's in?"

"I'll pass," Jamie said.

"You worry me, Jamie," Elisha said soberly. "You surely do."

Ed spread a piece of oilcoth on the ground and dealt the cards. Jamie lay on his back, listening to the game and the occasional nasty whine of a Minié ball overhead. Company I had made camp in a nice ravine, out of view of Confederate sharpshooters. That didn't keep the Southerners from firing in their direction from time to time anyway.

Franklin was somewhere over there. Jamie sighed, remembering their walk back through the lines after his painful discussion with Althea during the truce. They had passed first through the Confederate camps, and he'd marveled at how normal it all seemed. Men shaving, men writing letters, men nursing tiny cookfires, men lounging with pipes. Only their uniforms identified them as Jamie's enemy.

Then Jamie and Franklin clambered through the Confederate trenches, and on through the middle ground. They passed a group of soldiers—some Yankees, some Rebels—debating siege tactics. It was a spirited discussion, but not a hateful one. Further along two Northern boys lay on their bellies playing poker with two Southern boys, feet in the air.

"Franklin," Jamie muttered. "Why are we fighting this war?"

"I'm fighting to defend my home," Franklin said evenly. "Your army is battering a city where my wife and her sisters live. A number of women and children have already been killed. I'll defend the others with my last breath."

Jamie didn't blame Franklin for the edge in his voice. "You know, Althea and I always argued," he said. "But you and I—well, I'm sorry, that's all." He scuffed the toe of his brogan in the dirt. Sorry, sorry, sorry. Sorry didn't mean a dang thing.

Franklin had taken Jamie's shoulders in a surprisingly tight grip, and given him a little shake. "You take care of yourself, Jamie. It's too late for anything else. Just take care of yourself. You and me, we'll sort this out sometime. Later."

"Yes. Later," Jamie had mumbled. And as he lay in the ravine, remembering that bizarre afternoon truce, he tried to believe it.

Many Union soldiers dug tiny shelters like these into hillsides to protect themselves from the sun and Confederate gunfire during the siege. The white house in the background belonged to the Shirley family.

Courtesy of Old Court House Museum

Ziiing! A Minié ball ripped down through the oil-cloth the cardplayers were sitting on, leaving a neat round hole.

"Shoot!" Ed said. "That's my rain cloth."

"Two kings," Elisha said.

Jamie rolled on his side. He couldn't imagine "later." He was trapped here in Mississippi, in an army that didn't confine its fighting to battlefields, in a war that seemed to have no end.

— CHAPTER 16 —
Vicksburg, June 2, 1863

Althea

George walked through the kitchen door and spread his hands. "Bad news, Miss Althea," he said soberly. "Somebody done gone and ripped out every bit of that garden. Ain't a thing left."

Nannie, who was helping Althea sort through their dwindling supplies, stomped her foot. "All of it?" she wailed, and turned to her sister. "Althea!"

Althea leaned against the drysink, struggling to hold her tongue. Why look at me? she wanted to ask them both. Tell Caroline for once! She rubbed her forehead. The silence, after hours of bombardment, was deafening.

But in truth, she wasn't angry at George or Nannie. And she couldn't even be angry at the Confederate soldiers who, no doubt, had dug up the radishes and onions while the Bishop-Winston family spent the afternoon in their cave. She was angry at herself for being foolish enough to spend that endless afternoon dreaming about an onion and radish salad, dressed with salt, vinegar, and pepper.

"Hungry soldiers, I expect," she said, struggling to keep her voice even. "Franklin said they're at half rations. That's not much for men expected to fight all day and dig trenches all night. Well, let's see what we can find to eat. The Yankee gunners have to eat too. Maybe they'll let us get a bite in peace."

George emptied the ashbox of the Greenlees' iron cookstove, and built a fire, while Althea and Nannie poked through the pantry. "How about rice tonight?" Althea suggested. "And we've a tiny bit of that milk left."

"What's that?" Nannie pointed to the top shelf, where Althea had left the little muslin bag Jamie had given her.

"Nothing for now. Here." Althea handed Nannie a sack of rice. "Take this in and help Caroline get some water boiling."

Once alone, Althea touched the grimy bag with a tender finger. It held white sugar—something not seen in Vicksburg for a long time. "We don't need Yankee sugar," Althea whispered. That was a lie. But she was afraid to admit, even to herself, that the day might come when she needed it even more than she did now.

Althea was setting the dining room table when the plates she'd set out began to tremble. Mrs. Greenlee's syllabub cups began to rattle in their stand on the sideboard. We should pack those away, Althea thought—

Then she heard the loud rush and scream of a mortar shell, and the outside wall exploded. A deafening force slammed Althea painfully into the back wall. Instinct prompted her to fling one arm over her face, protecting her from the hail of plaster and board and wallpaper. Somewhere in the din was a woman's scream, the crash of china, a shriek of ripping wood.

"Althea! *Althea!*"

Althea opened her eyes slowly. Plaster dust sifted through the air like flour. Dazed, she tried to focus. Caroline stood white-faced in the doorway. One wall and part of the ceiling had been blown away. The dining room table listed into a yawning hole in the floor. The sideboard had fallen over, and bits of white china with gold trim lay scattered over what was left of the floor.

"I'm all right," Althea said slowly. "I'm not hurt." Her right shoulder ached like fire, actually, but she didn't think any bones had broken. Her fingers hurt too, and she realized she was still clenching a dinner plate. No. Half a plate.

Then she became aware of more explosions. Close. "Get to the cave," she managed, staggering to her feet. Some kind of black powder covered her dress, and she tried to wipe it off with shaking fingers. She heard George say, "Miss Nannie, Miss Caroline, get on to the cave...Miss Caroline! Get on to the cave!"

God bless George.

George shepherded Althea to the cave amidst a fierce barrage. Rushing screams of mortar shells ripped the evening air. The city's fire bells clamored in reply. Althea's legs felt like plum jelly by the time she staggered through the opening and saw—Thank the Lord!—Caroline and Nannie already crouched wide-eyed in the cave.

The four huddled in silence as shell after shell rained on their hill. The ground trembled. The gunboats roared.

In this 1890s photograph, a man poses by the cave where he sheltered during the Vicksburg siege. Note the shells lining the entrance. The door and frame were added after the siege.

Courtesy of Old Court House Museum

Althea's hands, pressed over her ears, couldn't stop the deafening noise. Pain stabbed her temples. Explosions quivered through her brain like an electric shock. Once she dared look toward the cave entrance and saw a bomb explode in the road with a burst of fire. Sparks danced and a jagged iron shell fragment landed near her feet.

The pounding continued as night fell, and as the dark hours dragged by. On and on and on. The incessant shelling rattled the marrow in Althea's bones. She couldn't see her sisters or George. Couldn't shout loudly enough to be heard over the deafening roar. Could hardly think.

But one thought did form in her brain with crystal clarity. When she had told Jamie that she wasn't afraid...that, too, was a lie.

— CHAPTER 17 —

Outside Vicksburg, June 2, 1863

Jamie

Jamie woke with a start, heart thumping, throat dry. The Union artillery was still pounding Vicksburg from the rear. The night sky flickered and flashed with the screaming shells. He cocked his head, straining to hear the other sound—the one that woke him—among the thunder. He heard another blast from the cannon. Someone snoring like a mill saw nearby. Even a lizard skittering over the canvas he and Elisha had fixed as a sun shield over the sleeping hole they'd scooped from the ravine wall. Nothing more.

"Elisha," he hissed, shaking his friend's shoulder. "Elisha!" No response.

Jamie sighed. Waking Elisha was next to impossible if they'd done nothing but sit in camp all day. This night, after hours of digging trenches, it was foolish to try. Well, the two of them had burrowed like gophers to create a safe spot to sleep. Might as well let Elisha enjoy it.

He heard mutters of conversation, saw two shadows picking their way among the sleepers. Jamie scrambled out and met Ed Houghton and Jacob Clark. "What you up to?" he whispered.

"We thought we'd walk up that hill." Ed pointed. "Get a good look-see."

"I'll come with you."

They made their way through the ravine and up the hill by the sporadic light of the streaking shells. They found more Yankee soldiers there already, watching the bombardment.

"I have to say, that sure is a beautiful sight," Jacob murmured. "I never saw anything like it."

The cannon belched a plume of fire with every round. Each shell passed through the night sky like a shooting star before arcing down toward Vicksburg. The mortar shells fired from the gunboats facing the city blasted high enough to seemingly mingle with the stars before plunging back toward earth. Some didn't burst until they struck. Some exploded in the air, scattering burning bits like blue and yellow stars.

Jamie clenched his hands into fists. "Can you hear anything?"

"Beyond the firing, you mean? Just the crash when a shell hits a building in town."

Jamie put his fingers in his ears. "I can hear something else." Surely the others could hear it too. It *wasn't* in his head. Not this time.

For a long moment no one answered. Then Ed shook his head. "That's fire bells, I think. One of the shells must have started a fire."

Jamie heard the fire bells too, but that wasn't what had woken him. "Can't you hear the women—," he began, but the artillery let off another blast. It was no use anyway. They didn't hear it. He slumped to the ground and leaned back on his hands, watching. Helpless rage trembled in his gut. With his own ears, he'd heard one of General Grant's staff officers say they would starve Vicksburg into surrender. So *why* did they have to rain death on the city too?

A flickering, yellow glare slowly rose from Vicksburg as the fire raged. Jamie pictured the city as he knew it, trying to gauge what section was burning. Was it the commercial section near Washington and Jackson? Or the more residential areas, somewhere along Walnut or Cherry or Monroe Streets?

He closed his fingers around a rock, squeezing until it hurt, then squeezing harder still. Not Monroe Street. Please, God. Not Monroe Street.

— Chapter 18 —
Vicksburg, June 3, 1863

Althea

Althea felt more dead than alive by the time the first shadows of dawn crept into the cave. She lay curled on one of the board benches. At some point Nannie had found her way into Althea's arms. Althea eased to a sitting position, wincing, and gently set Nannie aside. "Come on, Nannie. Get up. Caroline? George? Is everyone all right?" Dazed, they looked about, taking stock. Althea's body ached. Dust caked her throat, and her stomach felt hollow. But the shelling was growing more sporadic.

Squinting in the morning sun, they crept outside...and stopped cold, stunned. Althea stared at a dead horse in the road. A pretty bay, still saddled, now covered with blood and gore. Beyond the house, further in to town, huge billows of smoke roiled skyward from what was surely a mighty fire.

She turned away and led her sisters into the Greenlees' side yard. Rose bushes and arborvitae trees lay helter-skelter. Long strands of ivy dangled broken and forlorn from the wall. Bits of plank and shingles had been scattered around two huge craters made by unexploded shells. Somewhere nearby a dog howled mournfully.

George began hauling debris out of their path. Before tossing a torn rosebush aside, he snapped one perfect yellow bloom and handed it to Caroline. "Here, Miss Caroline."

Caroline accepted the flower silently. She shoved at the hair straggling down her back, and rubbed at a smear of mud on her skirt. Then, very quietly, she began to cry.

"Lordy, I'm sorry, Miss Caroline!" George exclaimed. "I didn't mean nothing—"

"Caroline!" Althea cried sharply. "That won't help—"

She broke off as another mortar shell approached. Shrieking, descending. Close. Too close. Which way to run? Althea froze, paralyzed with indecision.

Nannie bolted for the cave. She reached it just as the bomb landed on top of the hill. A few seconds later a muffled explosion blew clods of clay and a cloud of dust from the cave. The archway over the door collapsed.

"Nannie!" Althea and Caroline screamed. Caroline sagged to the ground. George ran for the cave. Althea felt blood surge through her veins and she ran too.

The settling dust revealed a landslide of earth and no Nannie. George began throwing soil aside like a frantic hound. Althea dropped to her knees, scrabbling wildly with her hands. Panting. Lungs burning. Something bitter puckering her tongue.

"I got her foot," George gasped. Althea saw a brown shoe, a striped stocking, a torn pantalette emerge from the earth. Then she heard Nannie's choking cough and almost sobbed with relief. Nannie wasn't dead! Within moments, the little girl was free.

The shell had fallen about six feet into the bank above the cave before exploding, causing the arched entrance to collapse. Nannie had fallen forward and been trapped from about the waist down. She spit out dust, hacking, weeping. A trickle of blood ran from her mouth. "Let me see," Althea said, using her petticoat to wipe away the blood and dirt. "I think you bit your tongue," she said, willing her own heart to slow its frantic thumping.

George ran his hands down Nannie's legs as he would a young colt's. "No broken bones," he proclaimed.

Althea pulled Nannie onto her lap. "You're all right," she crooned. "You're all right." More lies.

Finally Nannie's tears faded to shuddering sniffles. Althea helped her to her feet. "Can you walk by yourself?" Nannie nodded. "Well, we never did get supper last night," Althea said. "Let's at least try to find some breakfast."

Only then did she remember Caroline. Her older sister sat on the torn earth in the Greenlees' side yard, crying. "Caroline," Althea sighed as they approached. Her surge of energy had passed. It was hard to put one foot in front of the other. "She's all right. Do you hear me?"

"She could have been killed!" Caroline sobbed. "We all could have been killed!"

"Well, we weren't, this time." Althea felt a trickle of alarm. Caroline usually wept prettily, with wide eyes and quivering lips and tears dangling from long eyelashes. Now Caroline's face was blotchy, and her nose was running. "Come on, Caroline. Get up."

"There's—no—place—to—go!" Caroline gasped, barely able to get the words out. "We should have gotten out of Vicksburg, we should have gone..."

"Come on, Miss Nannie," George said. "Let's go wash your face, and find you something to eat."

Caroline fell over, burying her face in her elbow. "We're all going to be killed," she sobbed.

Althea sank down beside her, stretched out a hand, then dropped it. "Stop it," she said. "Stop it! Why do *you* get the luxury of breaking down? Why do I have to act like the oldest? You're the oldest! You're the married one! You're supposed to be in charge!"

"I can't," Caroline moaned. "It's all my fault. It's all my fault! I was the one who wanted to come here. I was the one who wouldn't leave. You almost got killed last night, and Nannie almost got killed just now!"

The fire alarm bells shrilled in the distance. Althea watched a little green-eyed lizard climb over her shoe. "I almost got Nannie killed last fall. In the fire." She'd never spoken those words out loud before.

Caroline sat up slowly. "You were trying to help me. You didn't know they were going to burn down the house. I...I just wanted to stay close to Franklin. I wasn't thinking about you or Nannie."

Althea turned her head as a shell approached—no, it was going wide. "You know what? It's done now. We're here. The thing is, we've got to get through this. Get Nannie through this, and George. They're our responsibility."

"I don't think I can," Caroline whispered. She plucked a petal from the rose George had given her. Another. Another. Althea watched the petals fall into a little pile and wondered if Vicksburg would crumble like that, petal by petal, until there was nothing left.

"Let's get something to eat," she said, because she couldn't think of anything else. "We'll feel better then. We'll be able to think better then." She lunged to her feet and tugged Caroline's arm.

In the kitchen, George had divided the last of the ham. Nannie had already finished her piece. We'll have to go to the market, Althea thought dully, but she couldn't face that right now. First things first. They needed to find safe shelter. But...surely that challenge was insurmountable. There was no safe shelter in Vicksburg.

Althea suddenly couldn't bear to look at the others. She wandered into the dining room. The mahogany table dangled into the crater ripped by the bomb, half-swallowed. Althea shivered. George could drive a hay wagon through the hole in the wall.

She heard an angry chittering, and stepped to the hole. A birds' nest lay on the ground, with three broken eggs. A swallow hopped back and forth nearby, while its mate called from a tree. Althea stared at the crushed nest and felt tears burn her eyes. *I can't do this*, she thought. I simply can't do this. If she could see Jamie right that minute she would tell him he'd been right all along, and beg him to help her get out of Vicksburg.

Althea sank to the floor. She sat for a long time, staring at the pathetic nest and crying quietly, so no one would hear. Finally she heard the courthouse clock strike eight. With an enormous effort, she got to her feet. She knuckled away her tears, and slapped some dust from her skirt. "Come on," she called to the others. "We need to make a plan."

By now Vicksburg, the city of hills, was studded with more than five hundred caves. Tiny fireplace-sized scrapes along the roads gave passers-by a place to duck into when shells approached. Room-sized dugouts like the one by the Greenlees' home provided at least dubious haven during the worst spells. But many families had already moved underground for good. The tallest clay banks boasted rows of large, multi-roomed warrens where multiple families lived.

Althea took her family to one of these.

"Is Mrs. Martin here?" she shouted to a group of women sitting under a brush arbor at the entrance, trying to be heard above the cannon's roar. "Mrs. Martin told me to come if it got too bad to stay at our house..."

Someone fetched Mrs. Martin and she, bless her, got the new refugees settled. This cave had two entrances, reducing the danger of collapses—like the one that almost buried Nannie—trapping the occupants inside. Near each entrance small rooms, or "galleries," as Mrs. Martin called them, had been set aside for servants' and slaves' use. Residents used a central room for community gatherings. Interior galleries were occupied as family dormitories, separated by partitions made of bed quilts or salvaged lumber. Mrs. Martin found an empty clay cell for the girls' use. "An officer's wife and baby daughter were living here," she explained, "but they left yesterday."

"Where on earth did they go?" Caroline gasped.

"The lady's husband took her to the front lines," Mrs. Martin said wryly. "He thought she'd be safer there." Her sad mouth turned up, wreathing her face with that unexpected smile. "Well, I'll leave you to get settled. I'm going to the hospital later, Althea, if you want to walk along."

"So," Althea said, after her friend had gone. "Let's think about what we can fit in this space. We'll need to fix up beds. And haul down something to keep food in—maybe that little trunk in Mrs. Greenlee's bedroom."

"We're going to live here all the time?" Nannie's face twisted unhappily.

"Oh, Althea..." Caroline wasn't crying, but she looked like she wanted to.

"It won't be so bad," Althea said firmly. "Didn't you notice how some people have fixed up their rooms?" They'd passed walls plastered with newspaper to ward away the damp, floors spread with carpets, separate niches where slave cooks scraped meals together on little cookstoves.

Caroline and Nannie stayed at the cave while George and Althea made several arduous trips back to the house, dodging shells and once sheltering in a cave with several other pedestrians for an hour when the bombardment was especially severe. By the end of the day the girls' gallery was floored with strips of Mrs. Greenlee's Brussels carpet. Tidy sleeping pallets, piled high with quilts and coverlets, lined the walls. One trunk held their meager food supply; another, spare clothes and a few personal keepsakes. Althea stacked a bucket, a washbasin, and a few cooking utensils in a corner while George fixed one of Mrs. Greenlee's parlor curtains over the entranceway.

"I'll fetch down that rocking chair you favor tomorrow, Miss Caroline," George promised. "And a couple of other chairs too."

"Make sure you fix up a corner of your own space with whatever you need," Althea said gratefully. Heavens above, what would she do without George?

"And you'll take a message to Franklin?" Caroline added. "So he knows where to find us?"

George promised he would. After he left to see to his own accommodations, Althea looked around. "There, you see? It won't be so bad."

Caroline sighed. "I think I'll just lie down."

Nannie slapped her neck. "There's too many mosquitoes in here! And I'm thirsty."

"I think there's a cistern out front," Althea said, trying to stem her impatience. "Let's take the bucket and go see."

Althea felt a fresh gnaw of worry when she saw the cistern crowded with both civilians and visiting soldiers. Vicksburg perched so high above water level that digging wells was impossible. Rainwater was collected in cisterns, instead—and clean water was getting as scarce as food. She and Nannie waited their turn, then started back through the twisting tunnel to their own room.

Unexpectedly, Althea felt comforted by the press of people. In between explosions, an unusual gabble filled the underground maze: a baby's cry, a mother's lullaby, laughter from what sounded like a game of whist, a quiet Negro melody. "I feel safer here," she murmured to Nannie. "Don't you?"

"No," Nannie said crossly. "I don't like it here."

Althea bit her tongue—actually bit her tongue—to keep from saying, Would you rather be blown to bits in the Greenlees' house? Or crushed again in that little cave? She rummaged desperately for something to say. "I think it's an adventure to stay here."

"I don't like adventures." Nannie's voice took on the whiny tone most calculated to drive listeners to distraction.

***Vicksburg Woman in a Cave,* by Adalbert Volck**

One besieged woman wrote, "I shall never forget my extreme fear during the night, and my utter hopelessness of ever seeing the morning light."

Library of Congress

Althea nodded to a twig-thin woman in a corn-colored dress as they approached the central open gallery. Several other women were gathering, with chairs and sewing baskets and candles that cast enormous shadows on the clay walls, and attracted huge whirling insects. A few children sprawled on the floor.

"Well, I think this is just like *Arabian Nights*," Althea told Nannie, wondering if Caroline might feel better for joining the sewing circle. Caroline needed to keep busy.

Nannie sulked. "I don't even know what *Arabian Nights* is."

"You don't know *Arabian Nights*? You don't know about Ali Baba's thieves, and the genii of the ring and lamp? That's exactly what this cave makes me think of. I'll tell you the story when we get back to our own room. This way."

Althea shepherded Nannie toward their room, but a young woman with an infant in her arms and a spitup-stained dress called her back. "Please—it's Althea, isn't it? Althea Winston?"

Althea squinted in the gloom. "Oh, we met at church, didn't we?" Drat, what was this woman's name? Althea glanced desperately at Nannie, who never forgot a name, but Nannie didn't get the hint.

It didn't seem to matter. "Please, if you don't mind," the woman said hesitantly, "I heard what you just said. Would you mind telling the story out here? The children get so restless. If you wouldn't mind..."

"No," Althea said. "I don't mind at all."

— CHAPTER 19 —
Outside Vicksburg, June 15, 1863

Jamie

The Yankee soldiers dug like gophers as the hot June days crept past, constructing zigzagging corridors that stretched for miles. Company captains picked out the best shots to serve as sharpshooters. The Oneida boys, who could just about shoot a mosquito out of the air, sometimes tucked branches in their clothing and crept forward so stealthily they were never spotted. Jamie and Elisha, average shots at best, escaped notice for this prestigious duty. Jamie was grateful for the body-numbing labor and mind-numbing routine.

Elisha was not. "I have a new idea," he said one afternoon, when he and Jamie were on duty in one of the forward rifle pits. "Watch this." He pulled a small mirror from his pocket, and wedged it in a forked stick. "I think I can rig this up so I can sit with my back to the wall, and my gun propped in place, and keep watch in the mirror. Then I don't have to show so much as my eyeball at the peephole."

Jamie raised his eyebrows. "Could work," he said generously. "But—"

"Hey, Carswell! Heads up!" Someone down the line shouted.

Jamie dropped his gun and threw his arms over his face as something whizzed past and landed with a thud in the clay in front of him. Heart hammering, he dared a peek—the Confederates had taken to tossing hand missiles into the Yankee trenches, but sometimes the fuses were so long they could be tossed back again before they exploded.

But instead of a sputtering missile, a rock lay at his feet. Someone had tied a dirty piece of paper to it with twine, and printed "Jamie Carswell, Company I, 14th Wisconsin Regiment" in bold black ink. Jamie snatched it. He recognized that writing.

"Mail service," Elisha said approvingly.

"It's from Althea." Jamie worked the knotted twine free carefully. The folded paper was stained with mud, and a bit torn. But readable.

> June 13, 1863
>
> Dear Cousin,
>
> George, who is well, promises to deliver this to the frontmost fortifications. From there I am trusting on the goodness of soldiers on both sides to pass this on to you. I wanted to let you know how much I enjoyed the book. I've read it three times so far, and would have started over if one of my neighbors hadn't borrowed it. We've moved permanently into one of the large caves, and live now like mice. We hear babies squalling, and family arguments, and yesterday the women in the next gallery woke us all when they discovered a rattlesnake coiled beneath their mattress.

But it is less lonesome here, too. We gather for prayer each morning, and at night some of the officers come in from the fortifications and bring us the news. They say you should watch out behind you, because Southern reinforcements are coming.

Nannie is faring better for being here. There are lots of children to play with. The boys collect Minié balls and shell fragments. The girls make mud pies, or play with paper dolls. This morning I found Nannie and a friend standing near the cave entrance, shouting "Go home Yankees" at the top of their lungs—did you hear them?

At night I often have a crowd wanting me to tell them stories. From memory I spin tales of Gulliver's Travels and Robinson Crusoe and Arabian Nights. At first I just had children come, and their mothers. Last night I noticed more than one refugee planter lingering in the shadows, and the drygoods dealer, and a number of the slaves. We all mix and mingle underground, you see.

The other thing I wanted to tell you was that the sugar you gave me also was received with great favor. The other evening a little girl was hit in the arm by a bullet. The doctor thinks she will heal completely, but it unnerved the other children as you can imagine. So I fetched my hoard of sugar, and organized a taffy party. I wish you could have seen the children's faces, pulling the candy by the flickering light of a few tallow candles, while one of the gentlemen strummed a guitar.

So you see, we are managing quite well. Why don't you give up and go home?

Fond regards,

Althea

Jamie folded the paper carefully and tucked it away.

"So how's your cousin?" Elisha asked, using his elbow to wipe a trickle of sweat from his forehead.

Jamie shrugged, waiting until the lump in his throat went down before answering. "Same old Althea. Stubborn and full of argument. They're living in a cave, now. Nannie, she's the little one, she's well. Althea didn't mention Caroline." That wasn't good. "It sounds rough. Althea said a girl...a little girl..."

He couldn't go on. Elisha's hand fell briefly on his shoulder, then away. Jamie nodded. It was good to have a friend.

That evening Jamie did some trading among his pards, then sat in the dust and scribbled a note of his own:

Dear Althea,

I received yours of the 13th a bit frayed, but in one piece. It meant so much to hear from you.

I have listened to the bombardment day and night for almost a month now, and can only imagine what it is like in the city. I don't know what will happen. If those reinforcements you are looking for don't show up, and my army takes Vicksburg, look for me. If anyone gives you trouble, give them my name. My captain is a good and decent man and I trust him to help me provide your family some relief. Always remember, my offer to help you and your sisters get away to my mother's care is still good. It is peaceful and cool in Wisconsin. And quiet.

Please write again, if you can. Warm regards to you and the others,

Jamie

Althea would surely be annoyed by that, but Jamie could only hope that some part of her might be willing to consider his idea. She had to be getting desperate. She *had* to be.

After finding his own rock and twine, Jamie scrambled out to one of the foremost spots along the entrenchments. He approached the boys guarding the spot.

"Hey Rebs," one was calling. "We hear you got a new general coming!"

The reply was startlingly close. "Who's that?"

"General Starvation!" The Yankee boys about fell over laughing.

"Well, hey!" The drawl was sarcastic. "We've been wondering. How you boys like the Sunny South? We're just holding on 'til y'all melt and flow right down the Mississippi!"

"Excuse me," Jamie sighed. "Do you mind?" They didn't. "Hey Rebs!" he called. "I'm sending over a pouch!"

"What's in it?"

"Tobacco! And some coffee beans."

A pause, then, "Whatcha want back?"

"There's a letter inside. It's for my cousin, Miss Althea Winston, in Vicksburg. It'll get to her if you can pass it to Colonel Franklin Bishop. He's on General Smith's staff."

"Deal! Send 'er on over!"

"I put a rock in too, to make it sail," Jamie warned. He hurled the pouch toward the Confederate line.

"Got it!" the Southern boy echoed a moment later.

Got it. For the moment, that was the best Jamie could do.

That night Jamie climbed the hill behind the 14th's camp again, and watched the screaming, scorching bombardment. The firing seemed especially heavy. The gunboats spit mortars like Fourth of July fireworks. The Yankee artillery answered with a pounding, deafening barrage that shook the hills.

Jamie felt the tremors shudder through him, deep into his very soul—whatever was left of it. He had listened to this day after day, watched the fireballs pound Vicksburg night after night, but suddenly, he knew he could not, *could not*, endure this much longer.

And then came the sound he dreaded most, carried on the humid night air.

"You know," one of the other boys said, "I can't pity the Rebels themselves. But it does seem too bad for the women and children in the city."

"Can you hear them?" Jamie gasped.

The soldier looked startled. "Hear what? The shells?"

"No!" A sheen of cold perspiration popped out on Jamie's skin. Nausea pressed soft against the back of his throat. "The screams!"

"The screams?"

"The women and children! Can't you hear them screaming?"

The other soldier shook his head. "Your ears must be better than mine."

Jamie wanted to cry. How could the others not hear them? "I can't make them stop!" he cried, and jumped to his feet. He gripped his shoulders as a shiver shuddered through him.

The other boy looked up at him, crinkling his forehead. Jamie noticed a few other stares directed his way. They think I'm going mad, he thought.

**Private James K. Newton, Company I,
14th Wisconsin Infantry**

In one letter home, Newton wrote, "In the night when it is still and quiet, I often go up on the hill and watch the mortarboats throwing shells into the city; at such time I can distinctly hear the shells crash through the houses. Indeed, some of the boys went so far as to say that they could hear the screams of women and children, but—their ears must have been better than mine."

Original ferrotype Whi (x3) 35806, courtesy of Wisconsin Historical Society

Was he mad? He'd heard screams at night long before the Vicksburg siege commenced. Or was he just more guilty than the rest?

Jamie took a step backwards. He couldn't bear their stares. He turned and ran down the hill, toward the artillery batteries planted on a nearby ridge. His brogans slipped on the rubble and he fell hard on one hip, and rolled quite a spell. Bruised, panting, he stumbled to his feet and ran again.

When he crested a little rise he saw the cannon batteries silhouetted against the moonlit sky. Saw the belch of flame, the recoil of the iron monster, the crew jump close to cool it down.

"Stop it," Jamie yelled. "*Stop it! I said stop it!*"

But they didn't hear. He ran again, trying to get closer. This time he tripped over an unseen log, and fell hard enough to knock the breath from his chest. He lay gasping for air, his cheek in the dirt, feeling the earth shake with every blast.

"Stop it," he whispered finally, when he could, although his frenzy had passed. He knew his army's gunners wouldn't stop until they'd pounded Vicksburg into submission.

But he could still hear the screams.

— CHAPTER 20 —

Vicksburg, June 16, 1863

Althea

The woman's screams ripped through the dark galleries, echoing among the explosions. Althea jerked upright on her mattress, heart pounding, and fumbled for a candle and match. The screams clotted her blood, and she almost wept when the wick took flame. She desperately needed that tiny glow to beat away the shadows.

"Merciful heaven," Caroline gasped. Althea raised the candlestick and saw both her sisters clutching their quilts beneath their chins, white-faced.

"I'll go." Althea poked her feet into shoes.

The agonized screaming went on and on and on. Other people were already ducking into the main corridor, bringing pinpoints of light like fireflies, murmuring. The story passed back before Althea reached the opening: a mortar shell had crashed into a nearby cave, killing a three-year-old girl as she lay asleep on her cot. Those who knew the girl's mother went on to help; the others went silent and grim back to their own chambers.

Althea went to the large room used as a gathering place, slid down in a corner, and buried her face on her trembling knees.

After a long while she sat up, wiping away a hot tear. Stubborn Southern rage poked at the fear. *You won't get me*, she thought angrily. *Or my loved ones either. You won't!*

She sighed, listening to the barrage. The Yankees kept to a general schedule, and she had learned to estimate time by it. She could hear the hideous clatter of shrapnel shells falling outside—the most horrid weapon of all, which scattered hundreds of lead balls when exploding—so it was probably about four in the morning. Sometime around seven, when she and George met to figure out breakfast, the Minié balls would start to rain down. Then the Parrott shells. Cannonballs linked by iron chain, called chainshot. Fireshells containing tow fibers soaked with oil, which kept the fire brigade on the run. Even shells filled with scrap metal: rusty nails, jagged bits of tin, links of chain. The shelling was always fiercest at dawn, when battery after battery opened, until every gun in Christendom was surely on duty.

Well, time to get back to her own gallery, before Nannie and Caroline started wailing too. Althea could still hear the poor mother keening and moaning. She had heard the laments before: when an elderly man was crushed in a cave-in, when a young woman was killed by a Parrott shell. The Vicksburg women's screams were the saddest thing she had ever heard.

Althea and George were just finishing their turn at a little cookfire outside the mouth of the cave that evening when Franklin arrived for a visit. Althea gave him a quick hug. "It is good to see you," she said, although Franklin *didn't* look good, not at all. Always lean, he'd whittled down to near nothing. And his eyes...they reminded her of Jamie's eyes, the last two times she'd seen her cousin. Like they were always seeing something else.

"Let's get you inside, and fed," she said firmly. "Caroline will be so glad to see you! And Nannie too."

"Yes." Franklin smiled. "But I brought you something, Althea. Here." He handed her a folded piece of paper.

Althea recognized the handwriting and felt a flush of relief. Jamie! He was still alive, then. Quickly she scanned the short note. Her toe started tapping impatiently before she finished. Drat that boy! Hadn't she made her feelings clear? How could he be so thoughtless? How could he even *think* about going to Wisconsin when she didn't know if they'd live through the night? And he hadn't even taken a line to tell her how he was faring!

She crumpled the letter into a ball and tossed it into the fire. "Come along, Franklin," she said, using a rag to pull their skillet from the coals. "George, you too. Let's go eat."

"I've done the arithmetic," Nannie announced importantly. "The Yankees throw approximately sixty thousand shells every day."

Franklin looked startled. "We try to do lessons," Althea murmured. "It fills the time."

"I'm quite impressed," Franklin said, ruffling Nannie's hair. He sat on a packing crate like visiting royalty. "At your calculations, not the Yankees."

Althea and George dished up the meal in the girls' room, which looked a bit homier now. Franklin and some of his officer friends had supplied them with narrow camp beds. George had brought a mirror and small what-not shelf down from the Greenlees' house. They kept jasmine and honeysuckle, brought back from Nannie's short walks, in a tin cup.

Caroline leaned over her husband. "Here, Franklin. Let me pour you some coffee."

Althea had made the "coffee" from parched sweet potato skins, and it was bitter, although Franklin accepted it gratefully. But when George handed him a plate, he frowned.

"It's pea bread," Nannie said helpfully. "We grind up the peas and mix it with cornmeal. It's nasty. But if you just eat a little, you'll fill up without getting sick." She looked proud of her knowledge.

So there, *Jamie Yankee Carswell*, Althea thought. *Even Nannie's not licked yet.* Pea bread was horrid; even the best bakers turned out biscuits that were blackened outside and lumpy-mush inside. But it was all they had.

"I'm grateful to have it," Franklin said quietly. He ate the pea bread, and the puddle of greasy mule meat stew as well. Only Caroline quietly put her plate aside, untouched.

After dinner the Winstons and Bishops played euchre with some of the neighbors. Then a few of the visiting officers sang for the ladies in lovely harmony, including one new ditty to the tune of "Listen to the Mockingbird":

'Twas at the siege of Vicksburg, of Vicksburg, of Vicksburg
'Twas at the siege of Vicksburg,
When the Parrott shells were whistling through the air
Listen to the Parrott shells, Listen to the Parrott shells
The Parrott shells are whistling through the air.

Oh! Long well will we remember, remember, remember
Tough mule meat, June through November
And the Minié balls that whistled through the air.
Listen to the Minié balls, Listen to the Minié balls
The Minié balls are singing in the air.

They received wild applause. The old ladies laughed and the young girls presented the men with wildflowers to tuck in their buttonholes. Nannie asked Franklin to dance, and soon several couples were bumping around the gallery. Another officer pulled out a handful of miniature fancies he'd carved from Minié balls dug from the entrenchments—a raccoon, a bird, a house, a plow—and presented them to a delighted flock of children.

The hollow ache in Althea's belly faded, and she felt her earlier anger slide away too. *Jamie*, she thought, *I wish you could see us now.*

Althea could tell that Caroline was trying to be brave. Still, Franklin's announcement that he needed to go brought the inevitable flow of tears from his wife.

Nannie ran off to a friend's chamber, and Althea sat in the common room until Franklin had calmed Caroline down. Then she got up to walk him back outside.

"Are you still going to the hospital?" he asked.

"Every day."

He sighed. "Just—just be careful. I know it sounds silly to say, under the circumstances, but—"

Althea smiled. "No, it's a dear thing to say. George usually comes too. It *feels* safer to have company."

He nodded.

"And Franklin...I have to go. It does the men good." And it does me good too, she added silently. She'd gotten used to going out. Much more frightening was the notion of never leaving the cave, of shriveling slowly like a plant that never saw the sun. Like Caroline.

"Are you holding up?" she asked him quietly. "I'm sorry we couldn't feed you a better meal. George and I tried the markets again this morning, but all we can get is mule meat—"

"I was thinking how lucky I was to have it," Franklin said quietly. "Some of the men in the trenches are eating rats, when they can get them."

They reached the cave's eastern mouth and paused, watching the Yankees' fireworks spatter the night sky. The percussions were louder here, and Althea had to strain to hear Franklin when he spoke again. "The men...they're half starved. They're shaking with ague. They're burned and blistered by the sun. When it rains they sit to their waists in water. They can hardly move without the Yankees firing, and they've been ordered not to fire back. The Yankees spend more ammunition in a day than we have left."

Althea mulled that over. "I heard that a courier got through. With percussion caps—"

"A couple have gotten through." Franklin turned his hat in his hands, round and round. "A few civilians have risked their lives too, floating down the Mississippi clinging to logs, or sneaking through the bayous."

Neither one would say the words: It's not enough. A mortar shell exploded in the sky, some distance away. Althea watched the burning pieces flutter toward earth like shooting stars. "Any sign of reinforcement troops?"

He shook his head. "No. Not yet."

A Negro spiritual drifted through the evening: "I wonder, Lord, will I ever get to Heaven—to the new Jerusalem?" A shell exploded some distance away, and a horse whinnied shrilly. At least there were no dogs left to howl. "Franklin," she said finally. "Do you regret it?" She spread her hands. "Are you sorry?"

Franklin put on his hat, and squeezed her shoulder. "I'm sorry for the suffering," he said. "But I've never been more proud."

— CHAPTER 21 —

Outside Vicksburg, June 23-25, 1863

Jamie

Jamie tried to stay away from the hilltop watching place after the night he'd admitted to hearing screams. For the next week he spent his nights dutifully working on the entrenchments, or curled into his hillside sleeping hole beside Elisha.

But one night he woke and tossed so fitfully that he feared he'd actually wake Elisha. Hot, sticky air pressed down like a wool blanket. His drawers had about fallen to shreds, and the heavy wool trousers itched like the devil. The shelling seemed heavier than usual. Did the gunners have special orders? After over a month of siege, they were surely so accurate they could hit whatever they wanted to. Where was the cave where Althea and her sisters had taken refuge? He didn't know. He had watched for another letter, ached for it, but none came. Did that mean?...

No good. This was no good. Jamie crawled outside, heart hammering, sucking air into his lungs. He couldn't lie quiet for one more moment without exploding himself. Better to watch the carnage than lie awake imagining it.

The 14th Wisconsin's ravine had taken on a gypsy air. A number of the boys had burrowed into the hillsides, shoring up the entrances with scavenged planks. Many had constructed little arbors of cane or brush to help shield them from the sun. Jamie picked his way through the campsite by the light of the moon and the endless flicker cast by the artillery barrage.

A few of the boys sat quietly on the hill, watching the bombardment. Jamie nodded silently to the shadowy figures and found a spot far enough away to discourage conversation. Almost immediately he noticed another shadow trudging up the hill. When that fellow veered from the crowd to join him, Jamie was first annoyed...then stunned. Elisha dropped on the ground beside him.

"Elisha? What on earth are you doing up here? Why aren't you asleep?"

"I came to keep an eye on you," Elisha mumbled.

So, the story had spread. Jamie felt his face flame. But he was enormously touched. "I'm all right."

"Are you?"

Jamie wiped sweaty palms on his trousers. "Can you hear the screams?"

Elisha did him the courtesy of pausing, tipping his head toward Vicksburg. "No. I just hear the shells."

"I can hear them, Elisha. I swear I can."

An owl hooted somewhere in the distance, and a few bats swooped overhead. "This can't last much longer," Elisha said finally. "You'll feel better when this mess is over."

Jamie tossed a pebble down the slope. "I don't think so."

"Sure you will. This is just particular hard on you 'cause you got family in there."

"This isn't just about Vicksburg." Jamie felt new sweat beading on his forehead.

"What's it about, then?"

Jamie opened his mouth...and shut it again. He rubbed sweating palms along his dusty wool trousers. "Elisha," he heard himself say. "I think I killed a woman."

"What?"

"Last August. Almost a year ago. I was on night picket duty. A fog rolled in. So thick I could hardly breathe, much less see. I got lost in a swamp." Cold beads of sweat popped out on his hot skin. "I heard a noise, and it spooked me something awful."

"And then what?" Elisha sounded wide awake now.

"I heard a voice. Nearby." Jamie's hands started to tremble. "I called out, but they didn't answer. *Twice* I called out. I had my gun up, and my finger on the trigger. I thought I heard someone take a step. And I fired. I didn't even think about it. I just did." He saw again the ghostly sudden spurt of flame through the night fog.

"Crimus, Jamie."

"Then I heard a woman scream. I swear to God, Elisha, it was the most horrible sound I've ever heard. It went on forever. I couldn't even tell what direction it came from. It was all around me."

A sudden burst of laughter from the other soldiers on the hill startled them both. The artillery roared. "What happened then?" Elisha finally asked.

Jamie wiped his palms along his trousers again. "Nothing. Absolutely nothing."

"You never saw anyone?"

Jamie shook his head. "I was too scared to move. I waited until dawn came. The fog burned off, and I was able to find my way back to camp."

"So...you don't really know *what* happened."

"I know what I heard." Jamie swallowed hard. "I remember thinking, when I first heard the voice, that it sounded like Althea."

Elisha was silent.

Jamie stared at the fireballs still streaking through the night sky. "I've heard that woman scream a thousand times since then. At night, faint, I hear it. It wakes me up, sometimes. I feel like—like I'm being haunted by a ghost." He gulped, grateful for the darkness. "I dream of ghosts too, sometimes. The women—"

"Listen here, Jamie, you got to stop this. The way I see it, you were just doing your duty that night. That's all. We've seen lots of hard things since coming south, but you just got to put that aside and—"

"Put it aside?" Jamie demanded. "Do you really think it's so easy? You don't know—"

"You think you're the only one's got memories?" Elisha sounded cross. "At Shiloh, I saw plenty of sights to keep me awake at night."

"That's different! That's—that's battle. This is women and children. Like on the Holly Springs march, when we saw that young woman get burned out. Althea got burned out, you know." Jamie ran a hand over his face.

"Did you tell her?"

"Tell her what?"

"About that night in the fog."

"Tell *Althea*?" Something twisted in Jamie's belly. "Lord, no. She's Southern! And—and she's already had a hard time at the hands of our army. I can't tell her I think I shot a woman! She'd never forgive me."

"You got to tell her."

Jamie rubbed his arms, unexpectedly chilled. He couldn't tell Althea. *Couldn't.* The thought of better times together, after the war, was one of the few pleasant dreams he had left. He couldn't risk losing that.

"You got to tell her. She'll understand, if she's everything you say."

"You don't know her. She—she's..." Jamie's voice trailed away. Althea was stubborn, proud—why, back when he was a prisoner, she'd given him a tongue-lashing just for enlisting!

"I'm thinking you've got everything, all these different women, twisted up in your mind. Once this siege is done and you sort things out with your cousin, you'll probably feel better."

And I might feel worse, Jamie thought, feeling very weary. No. This was one secret he was keeping from Althea. He looked again at the city, lit in the bursting flares of artillery shells. "Elisha, I just don't know what we're doing here."

Elisha bent his legs and propped his elbows on his knees, and rubbed his eyes. "We're trying to win a war."

"I thought—I thought wars were fought on battle-fields. Soldier to soldier. That's hard enough! But I can stand up to it. I never knew how much else got mixed up in it. I did *not* run away from home and join the army just to come to Mississippi and fight women and children."

"What did you join the army for?" Elisha asked after a moment.

"I don't know." Jamie shrugged. "You were there. Can you remember?"

"I remember working like a man at my place, cradling and raking and binding and stacking. I remember hearing my pa tell everybody at that war meeting that I was too young to go, and seeing Captain Johnson scratch my name off the muster roll."

"I remember something like that too. And speeches about the Union." It all seemed long ago.

For a long time neither boy spoke. The artillery kept pounding away nearby, and the gunboats tossed mortar shells into Vicksburg like confetti.

"I'll tell you something else I remember," Elisha said finally. "I remember that first battle we were ever in, at Shiloh. Remember that spell where we had to lie on the ground, while all those shells were flying over? I lay there with my nose in the mud, thinking of home, and what a foolish little boy I'd been to run away and get into such a mess. I would have been very glad to have seen my father coming after me."

Jamie nodded soberly. "You know, Elisha, a lot of the boys are talking about reenlisting when their time is up. I'm figuring on going home. You think so too?"

"No."

Jamie stared at the ground.

"I remember something else about Shiloh." Elisha paused. "We were going down a hill when someone hit me in the back with the length of his bayonet, and just about knocked me off my feet. Plus it hurt right smart. So I turned around to give him a piece of my mind. It was Gottlieb Schlingsog. He'd been shot in the forehead. He curled on the ground, drawing his knees up toward his head, and the blood kept spurting from that hole in his forehead."

"I remember Gottlieb." He was a German farmboy from Niellsville, a couple of years older than Jamie and Elisha. His father had made him wait 'til after fall harvest to enlist.

"That day, I just turned around and kept going. But Jamie, that's why I'm not fixing to go home 'til this war is done. I figure we owe it to Gottlieb. And all the others."

Jamie missed them too—all the men gone. Cyrus, and the others. Some died sick and shivering, some died quick, too many died hard. He ached to feel of a single mind with Elisha on this. But...going on, watching more friends die, watching more women burned out and starved out and bombarded into nothing...that wouldn't bring Gottlieb and the others back. "I need to feel good about what this army is down here trying to do."

"There's plenty to feel good about," Elisha flared. "They don't call us 'The Wisconsin Regulars' for nothing. We're fighting for a cause. Don't you believe in the Union anymore?"

"Of course I do! But—but I'm just not sure anymore it's worth all this." He nodded at another shell streaking toward Vicksburg.

"Then don't reenlist, when that day comes. The boys'll understand."

Jamie doubted it. "Let's head down. I can hardly believe you're still awake."

They began making their way back down the hill. "This'll end soon," Elisha said again, his irritation gone. "The Rebels'll surrender, and we'll march in and take Vicksburg. And you'll find your cousins, and you can talk to Althea. If they're living in a cave like you said, they're almost sure to be well."

Jamie shook his head. Talk to Althea? He couldn't believe he'd even get the chance. Surely anyone enduring such a siege would never be well again.

— CHAPTER 22 —

Vicksburg, July 1-3, 1863

Althea

Althea raised her voice so as many sick and wounded soldiers as possible could hear as she read from the latest edition of the *Vicksburg Citizen*: "'Grant's forces on Saturday made a considerable fuss, and for some time the opinion was entertained that a serious demonstration would be made on our lines; but the little good judgment they possess prevailed, and further than wasting considerable ammunition nothing was done...'" She paused. From across the crowded room came George's low murmur as he changed a wounded boy's bandages.

"Oh, keep reading, Miss Winston!" the Kentucky farmer pleaded. He did love to hear her read, or tell stories.

"I'm looking for another good bit," Althea said lightly. The next item was a list of Vicksburg ladies who had been wounded in the past week: Mrs. Major Reed, Mrs. Peters, Mrs. Hazzard, Mrs. Clements, Miss Lucy Rawlings and Miss Eileen Canovan. Most had been wounded by fragments of shell, although Miss Rawlings had been struck by a Minié ball.

These men didn't need to hear about that.

"I don't know how the editor manages to keep going," Althea said. The newsman had printed the current issue on wallpaper, since he couldn't get any more newsprint. "Let's see, here's something—"

An explosion rocked the building with such force that plaster dust sifted down from the ceiling. Althea squeezed her eyes shut and leaned over the nearest soldier, her heart hammering like a siege gun. She heard a woman's scream, shouts from the corridor. The hospital had been hit. Again. She didn't want to be around on Judgment Day, when the Yankees had to answer for shelling women and children and dying men, for it surely would go hard.

When the dust had settled she dared look around. George stared at her, making sure she was all right, before putting down the slops basin he'd been carrying and hurrying out of the ward to provide assistance. A few of the patients had raised on their elbows. Others stared dully, or twitched restlessly. No one in her ward had been hurt by the shell. Thank the Lord.

"Her ward," as she thought of it, had already been battered. George and a couple of the other men had only been able to partially patch a huge hole that a shell had ripped in one wall. One of Althea's patients was recovering from the amputation of both arms— one from a battlefield wound, one from that hospital explosion.

Althea glanced now around the crowded, scarred room. Many of the soldiers here were ill, shaking with chills and wasting away from dysentery. She and George had put all the cot legs in jars of water to keep lizards and insects from crawling onto the men. And she draped honeysuckle about to give the men something sweet to look at, and provide faint relief from the hospital stench. But there was so little she could do for them.

"Keep reading, Miss Winston!" the Kentucky boy begged.

"Yes," Althea said with a smile. She smacked a mosquito and reached again for the wallpaper.

Althea had exhausted the newspaper, and started on another installment provided from memory of *Wuthering Heights*, when she heard someone call her name. Franklin stood in the doorway.

"I had a chance to get away, and thought I'd find you here," he said, when she'd joined him in the corridor. He looked haggard, gaunt as a scarecrow, ten years older than a year ago.

"Aren't you going to see Caroline?" she asked, wiping her forehead with her sleeve.

"Yes, but I needed to see you first." He looked around the crowded hallway, and finally pulled her into a quiet corner. "I'm going to tell you something, Althea, but you must promise not to repeat it to anyone. Promise?"

Something flicked nervously in her belly. "Of course." She folded her arms across her chest and braced for the blow.

He leaned close to whisper in her ear. "This morning General Pemberton met with his division commanders and asked if they thought it was possible for our troops to attempt a breakout."

Althea suddenly felt cold. "You mean...abandon Vicksburg? Abandon the wounded, and the civilians?"

"No one recommended that we try it. The men have been cramped in the trenches for over a month. They're sick. They're starving. But the thing is, Althea, I don't know what's going to happen. We're almost out of food. The Yankees have tried twice in the past few days to blast their way through the lines with explosives."

"I know." Althea had seen some of the men hurt in those explosions or the bloody fighting that followed.

Franklin smacked one fist against his palm. "We can't last much longer. And one way or another, I won't be able to watch over you all. I haven't done the best job of that anyway, but—"

"Not one more word like that!" Althea blazed in a low voice. She tried to push away the words that echoed in her brain like a fire bell: *One way or another, I won't be able to watch over you all.* Her heart hurt, actually ached in her chest like a powerful bruise. "Reinforcements may still be coming. They *must* be! And I promise you, there's not a woman in Vicksburg that isn't willing to hang on a little longer."

Franklin smiled. "You are still a good friend, Althea Winston." Then he sobered. "And I'm counting on you to look out for Caroline and Nannie, whatever happens."

Althea pressed her palms against the wall behind her. "I'll do the best I can."

"It's too much to put on you, but I don't know what else to do."

"We'll be fine. We have George to help us, and Nannie's grown up a lot in the last year."

He fixed her with a firm look. "I want you to promise me that when the time comes, you'll find Jamie. Ask him for help."

That startled her. "I can't think about Jamie. All I can do is think about this minute, and the next—"

"I trust him, Althea. He'll do what he can to protect you, when the Yankees come."

When the Yankees come. She remembered a blue-coated Yankee insulting Caroline, smelled the smoke, heard the crackle of flames...All this time, she had marshaled all her energy just to get her family through the siege, day by day. Always aching for it to end. Worn down as she was, hungry and bone-weary, she realized that she wasn't ready to face the end of the siege.

But Franklin was waiting. She looked in his eyes and learned all over again how much he loved Caroline. And her and Nannie, too.

"Don't worry, Franklin," she said softly. "When the Yankees come, I'll find Jamie."

On the third of July, Althea and George were making their way to the market when a man with muttonchop whiskers beckoned her from the doorway of an abandoned photo studio. He ducked inside when a mortar shell sailed overhead, then popped back. "Miss," he called. "I see that market basket over your arm. I've got some flour in here, if you're needing some."

"Flour!" Althea and George exchanged a glance. Althea hadn't seen flour in weeks. "How much?"

"Just five dollars a pound—"

"You, sir, are a snake," Althea informed him coolly. She despised the profiteers, hoarding supplies and selling them at exorbitant prices while children and hurt soldiers went hungry. "I wouldn't buy flour from you even if I had the money!"

The profiteer's forehead wrinkled in confusion—
an odd reaction to her retort. But suddenly Althea realized too that something was terribly wrong. She stopped,
glancing sharply at George, and saw him hesitate as
well. "What's the matter?" Althea cried. She couldn't quite
place it. A dull ache began to nudge her temples.

George stood still as a fencepost, his knees bent
slightly as if afraid he might lose his balance. He
blinked, looking around. "Miss Althea," he said after a
moment. "They done stopped shooting."

Althea put a hand over her mouth. Stopped shooting? *That's* what this was? She had grown so used to
the roar that the silence screamed through her brain.
She had grown so accustomed to the earth trembling
beneath her feet that she was afraid to take a step on
the oddly solid ground.

She turned to a group of soldiers nearby, who
looked as bewildered as she felt. "Please, do you know
what's happening?" she asked.

"Some kind of cease-fire," one said. His left arm
hung in a sling.

"You don't suppose General Pemberton's going
to surrender us?" asked the one leaning on a cane.

"No! We can hang on longer!" The first soldier
turned back to Althea with pleading eyes. "Please, miss,
you got to believe us. We'd never surrender. We're
hungry, but we ain't licked. You can count on us."

"I know we can," Althea assured him, but unease
still prickled over her skin. This didn't feel right. "Come
on, George. Let's get back to the cave."

They returned to the bank of caves to find people
emerging like moles, blinking at the sun. Some smiled,
chattering happily. Others took cautious steps, looking

confused. As the quiet hours unfolded, some people milled in the streets. Others sat close to their caves, ready to duck inside.

"Maybe it truly is all over," Caroline murmured, as they sat on a quilt beneath a walnut tree near their cave. It had an intricate pomegranate design, stitched in the days when women had time for such things— how far away those days seemed! "Wouldn't that be glorious? Maybe it truly is all over!"

When the sun began to sink back toward the horizon Althea noticed George standing near the group of whites, waiting to catch her attention. "I guess we should have gone on to the market," she sighed, when she joined him. Althea hadn't eaten that day, and her stomach curled and cramped in protest.

"I think we have a bite or two left of that pea meal bread," George said. He shifted his feet, looking uneasy. The silence must be wearing on him too.

"I'd rather go hungry, just now," Althea said. "But Caroline or Nannie might want some. I'll ask—"

"Miss Althea." George stopped her before she could turn away. "Miss Althea, I got to tell you something."

Althea buried her fingers in the folds of her stained, limp skirt and squeezed. "What is it?"

He took a deep breath. "If the Yankees take Vicksburg, I'm fixing to fetch up with them. I ain't gonna leave until I know you ladies are set somewhere. But I'm fixing to go."

For a long moment Althea couldn't breathe. This wasn't real. He couldn't mean it. He wouldn't have chosen this moment to tell her such a thing.

But he did mean it. She searched his familiar black face, the calm eyes, the little scar near his eyebrow he'd gotten when they were both children, and he'd fallen by the woodpile.

"Thank you for telling me," she finally managed. She remembered how she'd felt when Flora, their cook back at the farm, had disappeared without a word. "And...and you know I want what's best for you." Her fingers jerked at the material they still clutched. "Umm, can we talk more about this a little later?"

He nodded, and melted into the shadows. Althea put a hand against the clay bank to steady herself.

Whatever would she do without George?

Finally she walked back to the little group gathered beneath the trees and plopped back on the quilt. Nannie and Caroline were both listening to a debate about the meaning of the cease-fire, and neither seemed to notice her mood.

"Maybe General Grant's just gearing up for his final assault," someone muttered. "Maybe they'll be fighting in the streets by this time tomorrow."

"I heard General Pemberton asked to meet Grant because he wants permission to let the civilians pass through the lines."

"I think he's protesting the constant firing on the hospitals."

Rumors. All rumors. Althea wanted to plug her ears. What good were rumors, when she knew for a fact that George had decided to make his own way in the world?

She remembered offering him his freedom, last spring, in a moment of guilty courage. After the Winston home burned, and she learned to live with nothing to call her own, she had realized how she had taken George for granted. He had chosen not to leave then, and she had been grateful. But the truth was...she had come to take him for granted again. Since he'd chosen to stay with them once, it simply hadn't occurred to her that he might change his mind. Not once, through all the days when he accompanied her to the hospital or the market, or dragged belongings to the cave so they'd feel more at home, or crouched over smoky fires cooking mule meat and pea meal.

Althea didn't blame George for wanting to leave. But she absolutely did not know how she was going to manage without him.

As twilight descended, the silence became harder and harder to bear. A few women tried to knit or sew. Children sat near their mothers in uneasy silence. The planters who had refugeed into Vicksburg from their plantations paced, and the slaves crouched together in the shadows. No one wanted to go to bed. No one wanted to sing, or play card games, or hear a story. No soldiers came to share the news. The oppressive stillness became a leaden weight in the hot, sticky night.

When people started rehashing the horrible possibilities one more time, Althea bit her tongue to keep from shrieking. Please, God, she begged silently. No more bad news tonight. Not tonight. I've done the best I know how, but if one more bad thing happens today I think I will simply break into a million pieces.

When someone approached, dislodging a stone with his foot, a woman shrieked. A man carrying a candle-lantern emerged from the shadows.

"General Pemberton has surrendered," he announced abruptly. "General Grant and the Yankees will take Vicksburg in the morning."

— Chapter 23 —
Vicksburg, July 4, 1863

Jamie

Jamie jerked awake with a cry. Or was it only another echo? The night was black, hot, and still as a grave. Was he dead?

Then Elisha snorted in his sleep.

"Elisha," Jamie hissed. He grabbed his pard's arm and shook it, harder and harder, until Elisha finally began to stir. "Wake up," Jamie whispered. "Wake up! I need to talk to you. I don't know how you can sleep with all this silence anyway."

"What?" Elisha mumbled. "Hunh?"

"I had a dream."

"You're always dreaming."

"No. This was different." Jamie flopped back on his blanket, wiping his face with a trembling hand. "I dreamed we were marching into Vicksburg—"

"In the morning, they're saying."

"—and at first all I could see was the rubble of buildings, everything smashed and destroyed. Lots of shell fragments all over." Jamie stared at the low clay

183

ceiling, seeing only the city as it had looked in his dream. "And I could see the ghosts, Elisha. The ghosts of the women and children we've killed. I kept looking at you and the other fellows, trying to see if you saw them too, but nobody else did. We just kept marching down Jackson Street. But I could see them. They stared at me. I could tell they were ghosts. Their eyes—their eyes looked right at me."

Elisha blew out a long sigh. "It was a dream," he said finally.

"I started to see women and children creeping out of caves. I felt so relieved to see them! But they all stared at me too. And you know what? Their eyes looked just like the ghosts' eyes did—"

"Jamie! Stop it. You're just worried about your cousins. You'll find 'em when we take the city, and then you'll feel better."

"I think they're dead." One way or another.

"All right, come on." Elisha began crawling out of their cubby.

"Where?"

"Let's kick up the fire and brew some coffee."

Jamie didn't want coffee. It was hot as Hades, and he was wide awake already. But he crawled after his friend anyway. Anything was better than trying to go back to sleep.

Morning found most of the boys in fine spirits. "It's Independence Day!" Ed Houghton exulted, as he tried to polish his worn brogans with a rag.

Jacob Clark was combing his hair with the aid of a small hand mirror. "I can't wait to get into the city. I might just march straight through and jump into the Mississippi, and take a bath."

"What do you think?" Elisha held a white paper collar he'd found somewhere against the neck of his grimy shirt.

"Fall in!" Sergeant Neverman bellowed, sparing Jamie the trouble of answering.

They stood in ranks to watch the Confederate soldiers march silently out of their works, stack their weapons, and march back. At least they tried to march, tattered and starved as they were. The proud, exulting Yankees fell silent. Jamie felt a lump rise in his throat at this unexpected show of respect. Not a single jeer, or even a cheer, broke the morning still.

Sometime later the 14th Wisconsin Infantry Regiment took its place in the long Yankee column and marched past the stacks of guns, over the Confederate defensive line, and on toward Vicksburg. A regimental band ahead of them played "Hail Columbia" and "The Star Spangled Banner." Thousands of brogans kicked up clouds of dust. Sunlight glittered from thousands of bayonets. The men hadn't marched in over a month, and faces soon turned red in the scorching heat.

Sweat rolled down Jamie's face and soaked his shirt, and his throat grew dry. Still, he had the oddest sense that he was still dreaming. He had been in Vicksburg less than a year ago as a prisoner, and of course had once known the city well. But this torn landscape was only eerily familiar. It was a place he knew—and yet didn't.

"You holding up?" Elisha muttered.

"Sure."

His stomach began hitching itself in knots as the houses grew thicker. Suddenly a wild cheer rippled down the column. Someone pointed to the gleaming courthouse on Vicksburg's highest hill. The American flag rippled from the cupola. "Huzzah!" Elisha yelled. Jamie opened his mouth, but nothing came out.

They marched through the outskirts of Vicksburg on the Jackson Road. The cheers fell silent. Jamie swallowed hard. Hardly a house had escaped damage. Some were little more than piles of rubble. Shrapnel balls lay strewn like giant pepper. Fragments of Parrott shells, mortar shells, canister, and solid shot littered the streets and walkways. Minié balls lay on the ground like ice pellets after a Wisconsin hailstorm, some flattened and bent. They had ploughed miniature furrows in Vicksburg's once-lush lawns and gardens.

Jamie stumbled and got whacked hard by the man in ranks behind him. Elisha gave him a warning look. Jamie nodded, but—Lord Almighty!

As they came into the city they saw the Confederate soldiers first, little clumps of ragged, gaunt men standing by the road, or slumped under trees. The Yankee column began to break. The Wisconsin boys scrabbled in their haversacks, and approached the men they had fought for so long with handfuls of hardtack, and sacks of dried fruit, and anything else they had to give.

Without the cadence of marching shoulder-to-shoulder Jamie's steps faltered. He stood in the street as his pards milled around him. And then he saw them, just as he had in his dream. Two women with armloads of bedding, no doubt heading home from a cave. And there, a handful of children clinging to their mother's skirt.

Jamie approached the family slowly. The little ones ducked behind their mother, peeping fearfully at him.

The Federal Army, Under General Grant, Taking Formal Possession of Vicksburg, July 4th, 1863, After the Surrender, by F.B. Schell

When Vicksburg finally surrendered, one woman wrote that she was "speechless with grief."

Author's Collection

The woman didn't move. Brown hair straggled from beneath a battered bonnet. Her yellow dress had once, no doubt, been lovely. "I have some food," Jamie said. He found several pieces of hardtack, and the breakfast bacon he hadn't felt like eating, and a packet of dried apples that his mother had sent. As he put them in the woman's hand he noticed how thin her wrist was. It looked brittle as a twig.

"I'm sorry," he mumbled. "I'm sorry. I'm so sorry."

The woman stared at him. Tears were streaming down her hollow cheeks. She looked exhausted, and heartsick. But after a moment she inched her chin a bit higher in the air. "You starved us," she said finally. "But you didn't beat us. And we aren't beat yet. Don't you forget."

Jamie watched them trail away like a mother hen and chicks, and felt an unexpected shiver of hope. Maybe, just maybe, Althea was still alive too.

Jamie couldn't remember exactly where on Monroe Street to find the Greenlee house, but he knew it when he saw it. A huge hole yawned in the west wall, and one of the chimneys had been knocked down. The ornate cast-iron railing along the second-story verandah dangled forlornly toward the street below. Still, the house was not beyond salvage.

He stared for a few moments, trying to gather the courage to knock on the front door. He didn't find it, and finally walked past the house. In the side garden, where Jamie had once squirmed through a visit with his aunt and cousins, George was stacking bricks against the house. Nearby a painfully skinny girl slowly picked up Minié balls and dropped them in a tin bucket—Nannie? She wore shoes that seemed to have been cut from an old coat, and looked more like a gypsy than the pretty, slightly spoiled little girl he remembered. But surely it was Nannie.

Jamie felt a river of relief. He might not have recognized either of them, for he hadn't seen them in three hard years. But George and Nannie were both whole. Alive. Jamie watched for quite a while. They ignored him, as they ignored all of the other Yankee soldiers out sightseeing, picking up souvenirs, surveying the damage. He wanted to enjoy this moment, knowing that at least the two of them were still well.

But then Althea emerged from behind the house. Jamie slowly exhaled his breath. She looked so much older than she had just last October! Her hair hung in a careless braid down her back. Stains marked her plaid dress, which hung limply around her ankles. But she, too, was very much alive.

"I'm going in to town to see if I can get some food," she called to the other two. "I don't know when I'll be back." The others nodded, and Althea turned toward the street.

Jamie stepped into her path.

"Oh!" Althea stopped cold.

He saw the sudden shock in her eyes and took a step backwards.

"Good Lord, Jamie," she gasped. "You look like— like a ghost!"

"What?" The absurdity of that remark left him groping for words. He looked like a ghost? *He* did? "What do you mean?" he managed finally.

She shook her head. "Nothing. I just...well...your eyes, I guess. You've got a haunted look about you, somehow."

"I..." He rubbed his forehead.

"And you're so skinny I could about blow you over. I thought your army was the one with food."

Jamie didn't know whether to laugh or cry. He couldn't imagine how Althea had managed to live through the siege. She was broomstick-thin, and surely scarred in ways he couldn't see. But she was very much flesh and blood. He felt relieved and stupid and confused, all at once. While he tried to sort it all out, she slowly stepped closer and folded him into a hug. She still had a bit of strength left, for a girl half-starved.

They finally stepped away. "At least this time you smell as bad as I do," Jamie mumbled, as he wiped his eyes with the back of his hands.

Althea snorted. "Yes, I suppose I do. Come on." She gestured toward the front step. "Let's sit down."

Jamie sat down beside her. A passing soldier was whistling "Wait for the Wagon" and Jamie suddenly wanted to whistle too. Althea had survived! With Vicksburg fallen, and Franklin a prisoner, she would certainly agree to let him help her and her sisters out of harm's way. He looked sideways at his cousin, shaking his head. "I have been so afraid for you."

"I know. But we're here. We survived."

"I saw Nannie, and George. And Caroline's all right?"

A shadow crossed her face. "Caroline...well, she's upstairs. I think she's just starting to realize what all this means for Franklin."

Jamie nodded soberly. "He'll be a prisoner. General Grant will probably parole the regular soldiers. He can't feed 'em all or transport them off someplace, I don't suppose. But the officers, like Franklin...I don't know."

"Yes," Althea said quietly. "I know. Franklin and I talked about it, a few days ago." She smiled ruefully. "In fact, he told me to look for you, once your army took the city. You didn't even give me time to think about it."

"My sergeant took me to Captain Johnson, and once I explained, he said I could come."

Althea picked at a spark-sized hole in her skirt. "I think Franklin was afraid of what would happen."

Jamie felt his cheeks flush. "As far as I've seen, there hasn't been any looting, or burning, or anything like that," he said quickly. "And Captain Johnson said rations are being provided to the civilians as well as the Confederate soldiers. Bacon, hominy, coffee, sugar, crackers—things like that."

She nodded. "Good. That's good."

"And Althea—Captain Johnson said he'd write a letter of passage for you." She looked startled. Slow down! he scolded himself. You're getting ahead of things. "I mean, for when you're ready. You and the others."

She spread her hands. "Ready for what?"

"Why...to leave. To go to Wisconsin. My captain said he can help arrange your travel. It's straight up the Mississippi River, you know. Now that we control the whole river, it will be an easy trip..." His voice trailed away. Something was wrong.

"But Jamie," Althea said slowly. "I don't want to go to Wisconsin."

"How can you not want to go to Wisconsin?"

"Because I don't!"

"But...what else can you do?"

"Stay right here, I guess."

He planted his elbows on his knees, rubbing his forehead. Foolish, stubborn girl! Finally he looked back at her. "How can you stay here? The house isn't fit to live in."

"Parts of it are. We're going to board up that hole, and then just live in a couple of rooms. We'll get by, Jamie. We lived in a cave for a month, for Heaven's sake!"

"But food—"

"We'll get by."

A Yankee officer cantered down the street. A group of blue-coated soldiers wandered by, pointing out shell holes. Jamie heard a mosquito whine in his ear and swatted it away angrily. "Look," he said finally. "You've got to face up to things. Vicksburg is taken, Althea. That means the Union Army controls the Mississippi River. That means the Confederacy is cut in two, and your supply lines are cut in two also. That means—"

"Hush your mouth!" she snapped, looking around. "Caroline and Nannie have been through enough without listening to that today."

"But it's the truth," he said, more quietly.

Althea stood up, rubbing her arms briskly. She walked the few steps to the street, stood for a moment, then walked back. She sat beside him and looked him straight in the eye. "I know exactly what all this means," she said carefully. "But you need to understand something. I'm a Mississippian. A Southerner. So are my sisters. We are staying here."

That wasn't good enough. He tried hard to find the right words. "I respect your feelings. But it's going to be so *hard* in the South."

"Harder than what I've just lived through?"

"Maybe."

She gripped his arm. "I know that Wisconsin is away from the fighting. I know there's plenty to eat there, and I'd love to see your mother again. I'm not sure how other people would treat us, but I could face that, I guess, if I wanted to go. But—I—don't." Her voice dropped another peg. "Jamie, I know this surrender may just well be the death knell for the Confederacy. And I can imagine what might lie ahead. But you know what? I can face it."

Jamie stared at the ground. A shiny green beetle crawled over the toe of his brogan. "Facing it might not be enough."

Althea nudged him. "I'll face it, and I'll get through it. Jamie, I can't run away now. My sisters, my friends, my soldiers—they need me. They need women who can still face what's coming. I can do that. And you know what? I'm good at it."

"And that's more important than being safe?" Jamie snapped.

"I've finally found something I'm good at!" For the first time Althea's voice trembled, just a bit. "All my life, I felt second-best to Caroline and Nannie. But I've faced this siege, which was more horrible than you will ever be able to imagine. I helped my sisters. I helped our soldiers. Maybe a few other people too. You have no right to be angry with me for that."

"I'm not angry." He felt more tired than anything. Here was Althea, close enough to touch—and she felt as far away as she had during the siege. A rock wall had risen between them, and he didn't know how to get over it.

She must have felt the same, because she sighed heavily. "Look, Jamie, it's grand to see you, but I need to see about finding some food for—"

"Althea," he heard himself say. "I think I killed a woman."

The confession hung in the air like smoke. Jamie sucked in a deep breath, almost as shocked as his cousin. In the distance he heard a woman calling a child.

"What?" Althea breathed finally.

"It was last August," Jamie said slowly. He picked up a flattened Minié ball and turned it over in his fingers. Stammering, sweating, he managed to squeeze the story out.

"You never saw anyone?"

Jamie shook his head. He couldn't look at her.

"Then...are you even sure it was a woman's scream you heard? Maybe it was an animal, even. Maybe you shot a cougar. Or maybe a rabbit got caught by an owl. Rabbits can scream something awful. So can foxes."

Whatever Jamie had expected, it wasn't this. "Or maybe I shot a woman trying to slip home through the swamp, so she wouldn't have to go through our lines," he snapped. "Or maybe she screamed when I shot her husband—"

"But—"

"For cripes sake, Althea, would you stop pestering about it? I was there!"

"Well, excuse me for trying to make you feel better!"

For a long moment they glared at each other. Then Jamie leaned back on his hands, smiling weakly.

"What?" Althea frowned.

Jamie shook his head. "I can't believe we're arguing. I expected you to—to tell me you hate me, or throw me into the street...and instead we end up arguing."

"Well, you're acting like a ninny," she said frostily. "Look, Jamie, what do you want me to say? What you described is a horrid thing. But you don't really know what happened. And that makes me feel badly for you." The annoyance faded from her face. "Anything would be better than just wondering, I think."

"You don't know what it's like, carrying something like that." Jamie sighed. "I've heard that scream just about every night since then. I felt like a ghost was haunting me. And then you told me about getting burned out by Yankees...later I saw another girl, she got burned out too...and then these last weeks, waiting out this God-awful siege...I'd go up on this hill and I could hear the women in Vicksburg screaming, too." He dared a glance her way.

But she surprised him. "I still hear those screams myself, sometimes," Althea said quietly.

"I guess I got it set in my mind that if I could get you and your sisters away safe, it would somehow help tip the balance a little. I'd know I'd done one good thing in all this."

"I see." Althea thought for a moment, then kissed his cheek. "You are a dear, Jamie. I appreciate what you want to do for us. Truly. It means more than you know. I'm sorry I can't do what you want."

He tossed the spent Minié ball into the street. The old loneliness was creeping back, filling his gut. What frightened him the most, dreaming of ghosts or worrying that he'd always feel like a hollow shell? "You just don't know what it feels like to feel so—so *guilty*," he burst out.

"Maybe I do," Althea said slowly. "I haven't told you this before, but the fire...back at our farm...it was my fault."

His head jerked up. "What? How?"

She told him quickly what had happened. "And Nannie almost *died*."

"But she didn't. You saved her."

Althea pleated her tired skirt between her fingers. "I couldn't save the house. And we were in Vicksburg through all this—" she gestured at the debris—"because of it."

"Then let's get away from all of this! You and the others can go north now, and I'll come along as soon as my term in the army is up. I'm not going to reenlist. We can..." His voice trailed away. She wasn't budging. He could see that in her eyes, too.

"I'm sorry," she said again. "But Jamie, saving me and the others won't make up for whatever it was that happened that night. You're putting everything on me. You think you'll feel better if *I* do something. Seems to me you won't feel better until *you* do something."

"Me? What can I do? You don't know what it's like in an army. I tried to stop things before, the officers—"

"Mercy, Jamie, now you're carrying the weight of the whole Union Army? I don't feel good about everything every Southerner or Southern soldier has ever done. But that doesn't make me want to turn my back on the South, either."

He stared at her, feeling like an eight-year-old again, trying to sort his way through some challenge his cousin had tossed at his feet. He wasn't sure what to make of that, yet.

But he was sure of one thing. "I'm proud of you, Althea," he told her. "And the truth is, I *do* know you'll make it through whatever comes." Just seeing her, talking to her, convinced him of that. Then he thought of something else. "And at least you'll have George to help."

Something flickered in her eyes, then was gone. "Speaking of George, I should see how he and Nannie are doing. And I *do* have to find out about food."

Jamie stood up. "I better get back to camp anyway. We'll be around for a little while, I expect. I'll be able to visit again. Tell George and Caroline and Nannie that I'd like to talk to them too, next time."

She hugged him fiercely. "Jamie...don't keep beating yourself for something you can't undo. You know what? Maybe, if you hadn't fired that shot in the fog, something worse would have happened to you. Maybe something even worse would have happened to Nannie or Caroline if we'd stayed in the country instead of coming into Vicksburg. The thing is, we'll never know."

Jamie shrugged, trying to smile.

"Let me show you something before you go." Althea beckoned him to a corner of the front verandah and pointed. A swallow eyed them from a nest balanced precariously in a corner.

"She's sitting on eggs, I guess." Jamie shrugged.

"Yes. Her nest got knocked down at least once during the shelling. I found her this morning, when we got back from the cave." Althea smiled. "Visit again when you can, Jamie. Whenever you can."

Jamie heard the courthouse bell ring four o'clock as he walked slowly back through Vicksburg to the 14th Wisconsin's camp, on a hill northwest of town. He felt strangely empty. He was overjoyed to find Althea and the others safe. And he even felt unexpectedly unburdened after telling her about that foggy night, and what it had done to him. Elisha had been right when he urged Jamie to talk to Althea about it. Maybe, Jamie thought, just maybe, he could learn to live with what had happened.

So why did he still feel so alone?

No...not just alone, or lonely. Elisha was a true friend, and he liked some of the others too. And he'd see Althea again, before the 14th Wisconsin got marched somewhere else. It was more a sense of...of hollowness.

He found his pards already settling into camp. Elisha was frying saltpork while Ed read a newspaper his parents had sent from home. Jacob squatted nearby, pounding coffee beans. Someone was playing a harmonica. Other boys had gotten a dice game under way beneath the trees.

Elisha shot Jamie a quick look, crumbling a piece of hardtack into the hot grease. "Did you find everyone well?"

"As well as possible, I guess. In one piece."

Elisha smiled. See? his look said. They're well. You can stop worrying now.

Jamie sighed, and tossed a pine needle at the fire.

"Carswell!" Sergeant Neverman approached. "Captain Johnson wants to see you."

Perplexed, Jamie followed the sergeant down the company street toward the bigger tents pitched for the officers. Did he want to ask about making travel arrangements for Althea? Jamie hadn't expected the captain to take that much of an interest in his family problems.

Captain Johnson stood talking to a lieutenant in front of his tent, but beckoned Jamie over. The lieutenant saluted and hurried away. Jamie gave his best salute too. "You wanted to see me, sir?"

"Yes. Something's come up. See that man?" He pointed to a big black man squatting in the shadows beneath a pine tree.

"Yes, sir."

"He walked into camp and took up residence. The men tried to explain that he has to report in town, like all of the other contrabands, but he won't budge. He won't say much, just mumbles." The captain spread his hands helplessly. "Truth is, I can hardly understand the whites down here, much less the coloreds. You've spent time in these parts. Give it a try."

The man didn't move as Jamie approached. He had the look of a field hand about him: barefoot, ragged trousers cut from shoddy, powerful hands and shoulders. "Hello," Jamie said.

The man stared at Jamie, but didn't move.

Jamie sat down beside him. "What's your name?" No response. "My name's Jamie," he added. "What's yours?"

The field hand's lips moved for a moment before anything came out. Finally, "Pete," he said.

"Glad to meet you, Pete." Jamie hesitated. He knew Captain Johnson wanted him to explain the rules about contrabands, and get him pointed back out of camp, but that seemed much too complicated. "Are you hungry?" he asked, and dug in his pocket. He had half a piece of hardtack to offer.

"Thank you, suh." Pete accepted the hardtack.

"Are you from Vicksburg?"

Between gnawing at the hardtack, Pete told his story in a few sentences: he'd been a field hand on a plantation near the Yazoo until the Yankees came. His owners had brought him into Vicksburg and given him to the Confederate Army. Pete had been digging trenches for them ever since.

"Well, you're free now," Jamie said. "And—"

A sudden burst of musketry spooked them both. Jamie peered toward the edge of the clearing and shook his head. A couple of the boys, still exuberant, had fired at a group of ducks flying impossibly far away.

"Don't mind them," Jamie began, turning back to Pete, but then his words died. Pete had turned toward the commotion too. Jamie could see Pete's black skin through several gaping holes in his ragged shirt. And that skin was striped with angry ridges of flesh.

Pete had been whipped. Not recently. But severely. Maybe more than once.

Jamie felt something sour rise in his throat. He had heard of such things, of course. But he'd never seen anyone whip a slave. And he'd never, to his knowledge, seen a slave who had been beaten.

Pete sank back on his haunches. "Thank you, suh," he said again, and took another bite of the hardtack.

Jamie sat in silence while Pete slowly ate the hard cracker. In his mind he saw all the field hands he'd glimpsed from a distance during his trips south. Chopping cotton under a broiling sun. Stooping along endless rows, picking cotton bolls. White overseers trotting by on horseback.

And he remembered the crowds of blacks that followed the Union columns through Mississippi and Louisiana. They came with nothing but the clothes on their backs, knowing only that the Union Army would deliver them from slavery. The officers, who didn't know how to feed and clothe and house the contrabands, as they were called, didn't see the situation quite so simply. But there it was.

And he remembered the man who'd asked him for help last winter, when Jamie was on that march through the Louisiana swamp. He'd been too frightened to even help that poor runaway. Had that man been beaten too? Jamie began to feel sick to his stomach. Firing that shot in the fog—that had been an accident. But turning his back on that hungry black man and his hurt wife...*that* had been a shameful act of cowardice. He was suddenly very glad that the Union Army was freeing the slaves. They weren't doing the best job of it, from what he could see...but they were doing it.

"Wait here," Jamie said finally, when he felt Pete's gaze upon him. "Let me go talk to my captain again." He paused, and tried to smile. "It will be all right."

Jamie was able to talk Captain Johnson into letting Pete stay in the 14th Wisconsin's camp for a couple of days—at least until he was rested, and fed. Jamie gave Pete that news, and sat with him for a long while. Pete didn't speak again, but Jamie was content with silence. He had a lot to think about. Finally Jamie walked back through the camp to find his friends.

"We were just talking about reenlisting," Jacob said. "You planning on it, Jamie?"

Jamie dropped in the dust. "My time's not up for a while yet."

"When it is, I mean. You get a furlough home, you know. And if enough fellows do it, the 14th gets named a Veteran unit." Jacob's eyes shone. Veteran status was quite an honor.

"I'm going to," Ed put in. "I mean, we took Vicksburg on the fourth of July! Nothing's going to stop the Union now."

Elisha nodded. "I'm going to, too."

Jamie shrugged, and they let it go. When Jacob dealt cards Jamie accepted a hand, but folded quickly. He was glad the others didn't press him further about reenlisting.

I need to be like Pete, he thought. Pete didn't know what his path held, but he had taken the first step toward creating his own future. I've been so busy carrying the weight of what I can't help that I haven't given much thought to what I *can* do.

No wonder Althea thought she was looking at a ghost when she saw him! Althea found her calling during the siege. Elisha found his on the bloody battlefield at Shiloh. Now Jamie needed to find *his* purpose.

Maybe he simply wasn't meant to be a soldier, and needed to find other ways to help out. Maybe he could become a teacher, like the ones coming south to help teach the Negroes to read and write. He knew Mississippi and its people better than most Northerners. That had to be good for something.

Or maybe the answer did lie in reenlisting. His army wasn't always one he could be proud of. But sometimes...sometimes it was.

Someone nearby began strumming a guitar. Ed won the poker hand, prompting agonized groans from the other players. Jamie nodded thoughtfully. He still didn't know how to fill that hollow space inside...but for the first time, he felt hopeful about figuring that out.

Elisha reached for the coffeepot. "Want some?" he asked, and Jamie accepted it with a nod. Yes, tonight was a night for drinking coffee. For the first time in way too long, he thought he might just sleep through the night.

Author's Note

President Abraham Lincoln once said, "The war can never be brought to a close until [Vicksburg] is in our pocket." For new soldiers from Northern states like Wisconsin, the Vicksburg campaign was a challenging introduction to army life. But men in both armies understood the strategic importance of that town perched on the bluffs overlooking the Mississippi River.

Jamie Carswell is a fictional character. His friend Elisha Stockwell, however, was a real fifteen-year-old boy who ran away from his home in Alma, Wisconsin, to enlist in the 14th Wisconsin Infantry. Sixty-six years later, he wrote an account of his wartime experiences. Although memoirs are often not as accurate as letters and diaries, Elisha's account is surprisingly detailed. He wrote about running away from home to enlist, his experiences at the battles of Shiloh and Corinth, night picket duty and routines of daily camp life. His memoir does not shy from or glorify his military experiences. He remembered clearly feeling "deathly sick" the first time he saw dead men, during the Battle of Shiloh. He also remembered thinking, as he lay on the ground with shells flying overhead, "what a foolish boy

I was to run away to get into such a mess as I was in. I would have been glad to have seen my father coming after me."[1]

In this novel, the troops that burned Althea's home are not identified, and certainly were not from the 14th Wisconsin. The entire incident, however, *did* happen to the 14th Wisconsin. Elisha described marching in Mississippi on a hot, dusty day, not long after the Battle of Corinth, and seeing a woman cut her well rope. "We marched a little past the house and stopped and sat down," he recalled. "The colonel sent his orderly back with four men and burned the house. They didn't let the woman take anything out—only what she had on. This looked tough to me, but it was war and it was a good lesson to her at least, and possibly to others." He also recounted the details from the Holly Springs march that so affected Jamie in this story:

> The boys that had been taken prisoner at Corinth were marched over this same road by the Rebs to Vicksburg, had been exchanged, and were again with us. They had been ill treated by the citizens. There was lots of foraging on this march and houses burned. The fences on both sides of the road...were on fire in places. The smoke was stifling. This was said to have been done by men that had been prisoners. In one case a woman had spit in one boy's face while stopped to rest and being exhibited by their captors to the citizens along the road.[2]

These incidents happened in 1862, well before policies of "total war" led to countless strikes against civilians. Another 14th Wisconsin soldier, James Monroe Tyler, wrote in his diary in May 1863, "Marched...through some of the best farming country I have seen in all of my marching and all of the nice houses and cotton gins were burnt on every plantation that we past."[3] These instances of burning civilians' homes may have been isolated events, but they did happen.

Almost all of the men involved in the Vicksburg campaign took such incidents, and the prolonged siege of Vicksburg itself, in stride. They saw these events as an unfortunate but necessary part of war. One 14th soldier wrote in a letter, "This is the ninth day that they have been trying to take that...devil like City of Vicksburg...Rebellion must be crushed cost what death or privation it must."[4] I based Jamie's feelings on Private Newton's comment about comrades claiming to hear Vicksburg women screaming during the bombardment (see page 157), and of course on the fact that his favorite cousin was in the city. But most men knew that the stubborn civilians could have avoided their suffering by leaving the city when they had the chance. Edgar Houghton, who was also a real person, described the 14th Wisconsin's ultimate march into Vicksburg as "triumphal."[5]

I decided to make Jamie's attitude toward African American people an emerging theme in this story because the Wisconsin soldiers' letters and diaries revealed that they were receiving an education while campaigning in the South. One 14th Wisconsin soldier seems to consider slavery only casually when he wrote in his diary in January 1863, "There was sum verry nice country & richly furnished homes but there was allways a lot of negro huts to spoil the aspect & ceanery." But in April, when an officer read and explained the Emancipation Proclamation, which freed the slaves, the same man wrote, "There was a number of strong speeches made on the occasion and there was the greatest enthusiasm shown through the Division."[6] Elisha Stockwell, who had not been concerned about slavery while growing up in Wisconsin, noted that after seeing two slave women being roughly used by their owner near Corinth, "my views on slavery took a change."[7]

Many of the former slaves looked to the passing Union soldiers for protection, and often a long column of black people followed the troops as they traveled. A 14th soldier named Daniel Ramsdell wrote of finding one slave at an abandoned plantation, much as Jamie does in this story. Once assured of their safety, the man collected a hundred or so other men, women, and children, who had been hiding in a nearby swamp. Ramsdell noted, "For a day or so they were very quiet, were shy about being near the soldiers or having any thing to say to any of us, but it soon wore off...They seemed to be happy but were bound to go with us when we left."[8] Many of the Wisconsin soldiers, especially the boys from small towns or remote farms, had never seen African American people before joining the army, and their Southern service provided them an opportunity to see slaves as human beings.

Althea Winston and her family are also fictional characters. The siege of Vicksburg, however, was remarkably well documented by the civilians who endured it. All of Althea's experiences in Vicksburg are based on accounts left by real women and children. Although Yankee gunners aimed at military targets, Vicksburg suffered horribly during forty-seven days of siege. A woman named Mary Loughborough described the experience of bombardment:

> Terror stricken, we remained crouched in the cave, while shell after shell followed each other in quick succession. I endeavored by constant prayer to prepare myself for the sudden death I was almost certain awaited me. My heart stood still as we would hear the reports from the guns, and the rushing and fearful sound of the shell as it came toward us. As it neared, the noise became more deafening; the air was full of the rushing sound; pains darted through my temples; my ears were full of the confusing noise; and, as it exploded, the report flashed through my head like an electric shock, leaving me in a quiet state of terror the most painful that I can imagine...[9]

Amazingly, historians believe that only about twenty civilians were killed during the siege. Many more were wounded, however. Shells struck playing children, or crashed into caves and caused collapses. Mrs. Loughborough added sadly, "The screams of the women of Vicksburg were the saddest I have ever heard."[10]

Emma Balfour was a real person, who with her husband hosted the Christmas Eve ball in 1862. During the siege she became accustomed to sleeping during the nightly bombardments, and took note of someone who did not: "Poor Mrs. Crump does not get used to it, and it is pitiable to see her at every shell jumping up and crouching with fear."[11] I developed Caroline's character to reflect what might happen to someone who, like Mrs. Crump, could not withstand the siege's terrors. Like Althea, however, most Vicksburg citizens evidently never completely lost their spirit. Families braved bombardment to attend church—even when the sanctuary was partly buried in rubble. Children collected wildflowers and pretty leaves to decorate their caves. When the editor of the *Vicksburg Citizen* ran out of newsprint, he printed his paper on wallpaper. Young women and visiting officers enjoyed musical evenings in caves against the accompaniment of screaming shells. And when the officers could not leave their posts, the young ladies rode out to the Southern lines to visit them there, traveling at twilight so they could see—and therefore dodge—the fuses of the approaching shells. Mrs. Balfour spoke for many when she wrote, "The general impression is that [the Yankees] fire at the city...thinking that they will wear out the women and children and sick, and General Pemberton will be obliged to surrender the place on that account. But they little know the spirit of the Vicksburg women and children if they expect this."[12]

The Federal Army took control of Vicksburg following its surrender, and although the initial transfer of authority was conducted with compassion, many local citizens were only marginally happier under occupation than they had been under siege. Black refugees—former slaves—flocked to the city, further straining its resources. Military occupation continued until 1876.

A visit to Mississippi today can bring the landscape described in this book to life. Staff at the Corinth Civil War Interpretive Center can provide maps for walking and driving tours. Vicksburg has changed quite a bit since 1863, but there are still a number of period buildings standing, and some are open for tours. The Vicksburg National Military Park preserves the Confederate and Union lines of entrenchment. The Old Court

House Museum displays a number of artifacts, including an invitation to the Balfours' Christmas Eve ball, palmetto stars made by children, and an oath of allegiance taken after the siege. The Balfour House itself, now a Bed and Breakfast operation, is open daily for guided tours.

Notes

1. Stockwell, Elisha, *Private Elisha Stockwell, Jr., Sees the Civil War*, ed. Byron R. Abernethy (Norman: University of Oklahoma Press, 1958), p. 18.

2. Stockwell, pp. 51–52.

3. Tyler, James Monroe, Company E, 14th Wisconsin Infantry, Diary Entry, May 11, 1863 (Madison: Wisconsin Historical Society Archives).

4. Heffran, Patrick, Company C, 14th Wisconsin Infantry, Letter to W. W. Willcox, May 30th, 1863 (Wisconsin Historical Society Archives).

5. Houghton, Edgar P., "History of Company I, Fourteenth Wisconsin Infantry from October 19, 1861 to October 9, 1865," *Wisconsin Magazine of History*, 1927, p 33.

6. Tyler Diary, January 11, 1863, and April 8, 1863.

7. Stockwell, p. 39.

8. Ramsdell, Daniel, Company E, 14th Wisconsin Infantry, Memoir (Madison: Wisconsin Veterans' Museum Archives).

9. [Loughborough, Mary Webster,] *My Cave Life in Vicksburg, with Letters of Trial and Travel. By a Lady* (Vicksburg: Reprinted from the original by the Vicksburg and Warren County Historical Society, 1990), pp. 56–57.

10. Loughborough, p. 131.

11. Balfour, Emma. *Vicksburg: A City under Siege; the Diary of Emma Balfour, May 16, 1863–June 2, 1863*, compiled by Phillip C. Weinberger (Vicksburg [?], 1983), May 27, 1863.

12. Balfour Diary, June 3, 1863, quoted in Hoehling, A. A., *Vicksburg: 47 Days of Siege* (Mechanicsburg: Stackpole Books, 1996), p. 95.

Glossary

Artillery—Cannon, mortars, or other large weapons, and their ammunition of shells, balls, or bombs. Also used to refer to the soldiers who work in teams to fire and maintain these guns.

Battery—the emplacement of one or more pieces of artillery, or a set of artillery guns. Also used to refer to a unit of artillery soldiers.

Bayou—a sluggish body of water that is a tributary of the Gulf of Mexico, a lake, or a large river. They often have no visible movement except from wind and tide. Term is used primarily in Mississippi and Louisiana.

Breastworks—protective fortifications constructed chest-high.

Cartridge—A complete charge for a firearm. During the Civil War, the charge was encased in a tube of paper.

Cartridge box—a leather case, attached to a belt or strap, for holding cartridges.

Entrenchment—to dig or occupy a trench. During the Vicksburg campaign, soldiers dug series of trenches which provided protection for them. Union soldiers dug toward the city until their trenches were very close to the Confederates' position.

Graybacks—lice. Also used to describe Southern soldiers.

Infantry—soldiers who fight on foot.

Minié balls—a cone-shaped rifle bullet with a hollow base.

Mortar shells—bombs fired from cannon at short ranges. They often exploded while high in the air, raining fragments weighing as much as twenty pounds down on anyone below.

Oilcloth—fabric treated with oil, clay, or paint to make it waterproof.

Pards—a term Civil War soldiers used to describe their close friends in the army, who had shared the same experiences.

Parrott guns—a type of cannon which fired an elongated shell; named for its inventor, Robert Parker Parrott.

Roesti—a traditional Swiss dish made from grated potatoes and onions.

Secede—to formally withdraw from an organization. During the Civil War a Secessionist was a person who believed in states' right to secede from the United States of America. "Secesh" was a slang form of Secessionist.

Sauerbraten—"sour roast beef." A traditional German dish made by soaking beef in vinegar and spices for several days before cooking.

Siege—an army's attempt to capture a city or place by surrounding it, cutting off communications and supplies, and battering it until it surrenders.

ADDITIONAL RESOURCES

Balfour, Emma. *Vicksburg: A City under Siege; the Diary of Emma Balfour, May 16, 1863–June 2, 1863*, compiled by Phillip C. Weinberger. Vicksburg (?), 1983. This booklet, available at the Old Court House Museum and other local outlets, provides a good example of a primary document.

Hoehling, A. A. *Vicksburg: 47 Days of Siege.* Mechanicsburg: Stackpole Books, 1996. The author replies on numerous accounts to present a chronological summary of the siege. A helpful resource for older students or anyone looking for more information about the impact of the campaign on civilians.

Houghton, Edgar P. "History of Company I, Fourteenth Wisconsin Infantry from October 19, 1861 to October 9, 1865." *Wisconsin Magazine of History*, 1927, pp. 26–49. Houghton's account is primarily a summary of military engagements.

[Loughborough, Mary Webster.] *My Cave Life in Vicksburg, with Letters of Trial and Travel. By a Lady.* Vicksburg: Reprinted from the original by the Vicksburg and Warren County Historical Society,

1990. This small volume is another excellent first-person description of the siege.

Newton, James K. *A Wisconsin Boy in Dixie: The Selected Letters of James K. Newton*, edited by Stephen E. Ambrose. Madison: The University of Wisconsin Press, 1961. Newton, a former schoolteacher, provided articulate and detailed accounts of his wartime experiences.

Stockwell, Elisha. *Private Elisha Stockwell, Jr., Sees the Civil War*, ed. Byron R. Abernethy. Norman: University of Oklahoma Press, 1958; 1985 paperback reprint. Unlike Houghton's account, Stockwell's contains many personal anecdotes, providing a good glimpse of the daily experiences and feelings of a young soldier. Suitable for middle school and up.

Winschel, Terry, Contributing Editor. "The Battle of Vicksburg." *Cobblestone*, December 1998. This thematic issue provides short, student-friendly articles and activities focused on the siege of Vicksburg. Appropriate for younger readers.

Voices of the Civil War: Vicksburg. By the Editors of Time-Life Books, Alexandria, Va., 1997. Because this volume is so well illustrated, and contains many first-person accounts, it would be helpful for students interested in exploring with primary sources.

Unpublished letters, diaries, and memoirs of members of the 14th Wisconsin Infantry Regiment can be found in a number of archival collections, including those of the Wisconsin Historical Society and the Wisconsin Veterans' Museum, both in Madison, Wisconsin.

Click on the author's website, www.distaff.net, to find additional resources for teachers and students.

To Plan a Visit

To contact the Corinth Civil War Interpretive Center, write to 301 Childs Street, Corinth, MS, 38835; or call 601-287-9501; or click on www.corinth.org to visit the center website.

To contact the Vicksburg Convention Center, write to 1600 Mulberry Street, Post Office Box 110, Vicksburg, MS, 39181; or call 601-630-2929 or 1-800-221-3536; or click on www.vccmeet.com to visit the center website.

To contact the Vicksburg National Military Park, 3201 Clay Street, Vicksburg, MS, 39183-3495; or call 601-636-0583; or click on www.nps.gov/vick to visit the park website.

To contact the Old Court House Museum and Eva W. Davis Memorial, write to 1008 Cherry Street, Vicksburg, MS, 39183; or call 601-636-0741; or click on www.oldcourthouse.org to visit the museum website.

To contact the Balfour House Bed & Breakfast and Historic Home Tour, write to 1002 Crawford Street, P.O. Box 781, Vicksburg, MS, 39181; or call 601-638-7113 or 1-800-294-7113; or click on www.balfourhouse.com to visit the house website.